# ABOUT TIME

by

## Paul Chapman

Dedication:

To my family that I cherish more than anything. Thank you for supporting my endeavors over the years, to my wife, that put up with my craziness and managed our tattoo studio. Managing a tattoo studio is like herding cats. Thanks to all my tattoo artist friends, I tried to be as truthful as possible. I know I left out some wild stories that we all know happened, but sometimes those events are just too unbelievable. I know I smashed some of the stories together; I am sorry.

**ISBN:** 9798422637362
**Imprint:** Independently published

# One

I think I locked the door. "Damn it," I walk back to the door and check it. I think

I am becoming obsessive-compulsive about this whole door-locking thing. The parking

lot looks extra dark tonight. It seems like more streetlights are out than usual. I look up

and down the street, and sure enough, all the streetlights are out. People are screaming

on the darkened corner, and there amid water from a broken hydrant is a Chevy Tahoe

with its occupants arguing. The lights of the corner store are out as well. I can hear

sirens off in the distance as the first responders hurry to the accident. I walk towards the

accident at the corner; I see a body lying in the middle of the road face down in the

growing lake. The two men are running down the street, away from the sound of sirens.

There are no other cars around at this time of night. I walk towards the body. I can see

the red of the blood coming from a hole in his face. A gun is next to his hand. There are

holes in the front windshield of the Tahoe. Water rains down on the hood. The back

window of the Tahoe is busted, and I can see the bundles in the back of the vehicle. I run

to the Tahoe and reach inside to see what the bundles might be.

Without thinking, I picked one up. It is wrapped in plastic and is heavy and stiff. I take a

black duffel bag and run back across the street and around the side of my building,

where I stash the heavy bundles. I open the back door to my building and go inside. My electricity is out now as well. I go outside, get the packages and bring them in.  I lock the doors, then change my shirt to a bright yellow company T-shirt. I find a flashlight and knife and cut open the duffel bag to find what looks like money wrapped in rectangles.  I cut a package and found some cash. My hands are shaking so hard I can hardly cut the package.  I cut open the square bundle that was outside of the duffel bag. I found what looked like two reams of paper.  I find a white hard-packed substance inside this package, and I can only think it is cocaine.  The sirens outside are getting loud enough to be heard inside my building now. I open the first package from the duffel bag and discover six rows of hundreds.  Each row is about a foot long and makes a rectangle of cash the size of a grocery bag. I am all sweaty as I open the second package and find six rows of hundred-dollar bills.  The smell of cocaine is getting heavy.

I got some plastic wrap and duct tape to seal it back up.  I open the end of one row of hundreds, and it seems to pop like snakes-in-a-can to my horror!  Thirty-hundred-dollar bills lay on the counter.  I put three bills in my pocket and stuff the rest in the bottom of my toolbox in my tattoo booth, and lock my toolbox.  The duffel bag is too full, and I cannot fit the cocaine. So I lock them both in the storage cabinet in the back room.  I pull a chair up by the front door and stare across the street at the circus of first responders. A police car with flashing lights pulls into my parking lot.  He gets out and walks up to the front door of the shop.  My heart is racing as I fumble for my keys.  I pulled the chair back away from the door and waited for the officer to knock.  I take my time to open the door. The officer was walking back to the car when I opened the door.

"Hey, can I help you?" I try to act calmly.

"Yeah, did you see the accident?" The officer shines a flashlight into my face.

"Nah. I was in the back of my shop when the lights went out."

"Did you see or hear anything?"

"Nope. I was here. In the back. Umm."

"You, okay?  Is there someone here with you?  Are you okay?"

"Huh? Am I okay? What?"

"I mean, you are acting kind of weird, buddy.  Is someone holding you hostage or something?"  The officer walks closer with his hand on his pistol.  "Are you high or something?"

"No, sir.  I am just confused about what you meant, and I am the only one here."

"Did you see anyone run through your parking lot?"

"No, sir.  There are wrecks here all the time.  So, this is no big thing."  I try to be calm about the wreck.  Indeed, crashes happen there all the time.  However, crashes with bodies out in the street don't happen very often.

"So. You did not hear the crash or see anyone run through the parking lot?"  The officer begins to relax and takes his hand off the pistol, and he lowers the flashlight.  "Sorry to bother you, sir."

"So, what happened?  Were they on their phone or something?"  I tried to start a conversation, and the officer told me about the body out in the street next to the truck. He tells me I should not go in that direction to go home, and he tells me the intersection should be closed until the morning.  When I ask why he tells me the driver died at the scene and is waiting for the coroner and traffic investigation team.  We say our goodbyes, and he leaves down the street next to the shop.  I go back inside, lock all the doors, and make sure everything is clean.  I decided I should move the packages to my safe at home.  I take the packages, load them in my truck, lock up the shop, and drive home.

The drive home is the most stressful drive I have ever had in my life.  I just knew I was going to get pulled over.  I pulled inside my garage, closed the garage door, and then got out of the truck.  I open the back door to the house and prop it open.  I open my safe inside my closet under the stairs.  I get the packages out of the truck and stuff them in the safe.  I decided that I should go and get myself a bottle of Johnny Walker Blue Label Scotch.  I jumped back in the truck and headed over to the nearest Bev Mo store.  The girl at the counter knows me, and we smile and chat for a minute before I ask her to get me a bottle of Blue Label.  She brings it back and rings it up.  I took my prize home to have a glass of scotch and watch a movie.

I wake up, and the television is still on the menu screen of the movie.  My mouth is as dry as the desert.  I stumble into the kitchen to get a glass of water.  I drink it down and go outside to get my newspaper.  I picked up the newspaper, and on the front page of the paper is a picture of the Tahoe with water raining down on it. The headline reads, "Cartel Violence Hits South-Side."  I picked up the paper and read the facts of what happened.  Supposedly, the driver had been shot around midnight, two blocks away from the crash.  He had made a run for it but crashed into the hydrant.  Several suspects were seen running from the accident.  The Tahoe had knocked out the power to the entire neighborhood.  According to the paper, the street remained closed until morning, and the power would be restored by noon. The Tahoe carried 19 kilos of cocaine and one rectangular bundle of one hundred twenty thousand.  Law enforcement contacted the

FBI, which said this was most likely a cartel drug deal gone wrong.  The top of my head

was hot from the morning sun as I Stood there reading over the paper.

The clock on the stove says it is noon.  I can be late today or not even show up.  I

open the safe and pull out one rectangular bundle of cash.  I sit it on my kitchen table

and start to open it up.  Each of the six rows is a separate row of cash sealed tight.  I

count one row.  It comes out to two hundred thousand.  Twelve strapped stacks of ten

thousand; this bundle comes out to eight-hundred-thousand.  I keep thinking that can't

be right.  That means it is almost one-million-five-hundred-thousand here.

I sit back and try to think about it.  Now I am starting to get scared.  This is cartel money

and cocaine.  C A R T E L money and drugs.  They are more intelligent than the FBI.  They

will find out that I took that stuff.  What the hell was I thinking?  I'm staring at the stack

of cash when the phone rings.  It is the shop.  I let it go to voicemail, and they are

wondering where I am.  I put the cash into the safe, washed my face, changed clothes,

and left for the shop.  I look at the clock in the truck as I drive to the shop, and it says an

accusing four pm.  I have wasted the whole day staring at the cash.  The phone rings

again.  It is the shop; something must be wrong for them to keep calling.

I answer it, "Hey, wats up?"

"Did you have a busy night after we left?"  John, my shop manager, asks me.

"Why? I asked, and I did have someone come by. Why?"  I am beginning to get worried.

"Well, Troy had to get into your tool cabinet to borrow your armature bar alignment tool,

but it was locked, so I unlocked it."  John asks me again, "So, you must have been busy."

"Why do you say that" and his following answer wakes me up.

"Because you didn't fill out any paperwork, and there was almost three grand in your drawer." John is strict about paperwork, and I can hear the irritation in his voice.

"Oh, yeah, um, sorry, I will tell you when I get there. I am on my way." I hang up and try to think of a story that will be believable. I can't believe that I left all that cash in my drawer. Man, if I am going to make it through this, I will have to start paying attention to details. I think about the crash, which should be the day's topic at the shop and the store across the street. I could say that I found it on the side of the building after the crash because the police thought someone had run through the parking lot. I thought about it more and tried to come up with some reason for not telling them that story. It occurred to me that the story would put someone in the parking lot, and I had told the police that I did not see anything. I tried to think of something else to tell them. I figured that I would tell them that a friend had come by and dropped it off so his wife wouldn't find it. That was a lame enough story to work. My buddy Samuel was newly married, and everyone knows his wife runs his shit. I pulled into the parking lot of the shop. There were six people out front smoking and sitting on our benches.

"Hey, Dickhead, your wife John is pissy," Susan starts laughing, and she sticks her tongue out at me.

"Chris. Did you hear about that crash on the corner?" Troy looks at me with his cigarette hanging out of his mouth.

"Yeah. I was still here when it happened. The cops came by to talk to me about it." I walk past them and into the shop. There are tattoo machines buzzing and people in the waiting area. George and Rick are tattooing in their booths, and John is scowling at the front counter.

"Where is the paperwork, man?  You know how I hate to be making up paperwork for you," John is distraught.  I guess he has a reason, as I am the worst at paperwork.  I hired John to manage the shop because I could not seem to keep my shit together.  Since he took over, the shop seemed to flourish.  Everyone stayed on point, and John ended up the scapegoat for being strict, and I didn't have to do that anymore.  He is an excellent manager.

"Can I talk to you in my booth?" I keep walking towards the back.  John sighs and follows me to my booth in the back.  "Listen, John; I need you to keep this a secret.  Makeup whatever you want about it, but keep it quiet, okay."

"What.  What do you want me to keep quiet?"  He is now interested in my story, my reason.

"You remember my buddy Samuel that just got married?"

"Oh, yeah, Sam.  The whipped guy."

"Yeah, that guy.  Well, he dropped by late last night.  He has this wad of cash, and he is frantic.  He asks me to keep it for a bit because he doesn't want his wife to know about it."

John interrupts, "before or after the accident?"

"Huh?" Stunned. I had not expected this.  I think about it.

     "That's what I thought. I smell bullshit.  Why, do you have to give me such a pain in the ass," John is starting to get wound up, and he is agitated and begins to leave my booth before I can finish.

"No, man. Hold on there. I swear to God.  Look, he came in late last night.  It had to be right before the crash.  You had left, and he pulled in right after you left.  He must have passed you up. Anyway, he comes in, doesn't stay long, drops the cash, and bounces. His wife was waiting for him over at her mom's house or something." I look at John to pull him into the story. "Long story short, he drops off the cash and leaves."

"So, when did the crash happen? Did you see it?"

"No, I didn't see it. I locked up and went to the back to clean up. Next thing I know, a cop is banging on the door," I look up to see if he is still into the story. "So, I go open the door, and he starts grilling me like I was the one that caused the wreck. Come to find out, the guy driving was shot. I read that part in the paper today."

"Wow. No wonder the intersection was still closed off this morning when I got here at eight am. I came in early to sort out the paperwork and get quarterly's ready. I cleaned and mopped the shop. I called you several times, but you didn't answer."

"Yeah. I drank a bit when I got home last night and woke up on the couch. I got up and came straight here to the shop because you sounded like there was an emergency." Someone up front calls for John, "Coming. I will be right there. Jesus, you would think these guys just started working at a tattoo shop." John takes off and goes upfront to take care of the customer at the counter. I stay in the back and pull out the cash and count it. There are twenty-three hundred dollar bills. I thought it was three thousand, but I guess I was so excited that I miscounted. I put it into a machine bag with a rubber band around it. I turn on my light table and draw for my next appointment. Drawing seems to calm me down better than any drug. I think about all that happened the night before. I try to map out what happened. Had I heard the crash? I didn't remember hearing it. I had just finished locking up the shop. I was smoking a cigarette before I got into my truck when I noticed the screaming across the street. I could not remember what time.  I remember all the lights were out.  Maybe the crash happened when I went to set the alarm.  I generally turn off the lights then set the alarm.  The crash must have happened as I made my way back up front to lock up.  That would explain the yelling and screaming.  I remember there were no other cars when I went to see what had happened.  The clerk in the store had called 911.  Had they seen me?  It would have been dark, and I would have been hard to see, but what if they had seen me?  Would they tell anyone?

I catch a walk-in tattoo that is going to take five hours. Cha-ching! Easy money, and I spend an hour drawing and then start the tattoo. My client is a real cowboy from Oakdale, California. We talk about what he does for a living and what the girls are like in Oakdale. He says he likes LA women better. He says LA women are easier to pull. We both laughed at that. We finished the tattoo, and I decided to go to the store to see what they knew.

I walked up front and told John I was going to the store, and I would be right back.  The store is on the other side of a canal that blocks the view of the intersection.  I walk to the corner and stand at the light, waiting for the light to change.  The city crew had replaced the hydrant last night, and everything was cleaned up like it never happened.  There were paint marks on the street where the truck and body were located.  The light changes and I walk over to the store.  The counter guy Gary was not there; instead, it was a chick.  I glance at her name tag, Clara.

"Where is Gary?" I asked her.

"Gary comes to work at eleven am.  Who are you?"

"Sorry, I am Chris from across the street at the tattoo shop.  When did you get hired?"

"Last week. I have been working nights for the last three days. This place is crazy!"

"Really? I think it is calm around here." I shrug and walk over to get an energy drink.

"Well, it was crazy last night. A truck crashed into the fire hydrant and knocked out the power. Then some crazy-ass Mexicans start fighting in the street. They grab a bunch of shit out of the truck and take off running with all they can carry. I called 911 and hid behind the counter because they had rifles and shit."

"Wow. That is crazy. Did you see anything else?"

"No. The cops said that one guy was dead out in the middle of the street. I guess he was shot, and that is why they crashed. The cops found a bunch of drugs in the truck too."

"Yeah, that sounds pretty crazy. So, Gary missed the whole thing, huh?"

"Yeah. I guess. Did I mention that Gary is working the day shift?"

I paid for my energy drink and walked back to the shop. I felt a lot better about taking the cash now. No one seems to have seen me run across the street because the fountain of water from the hydrant blocked the view and the cameras. I guess I didn't run across the street cause cash and drugs were heavy. I must have looked like someone looting a store during a riot. I chugged my energy drink and put the can in the ashtray out in front of the shop. I feel so much better now. A big wave of energy and relaxation swept over me. I had to remember to keep calm and not use the money.

I would have to figure out what to do with the cocaine. It was the most I had ever seen in my life. Two whole kilos of cocaine- almost four and a half pounds! Jesus. I didn't know anyone that could deal with that much cocaine. I thought about it more. Damn, don't I have to cut that too? I didn't know what to do with cocaine-like that right out of a fresh kilo. I started to think about googling it, but then I thought I would get caught if someone looked at my computer traffic.  Damn, I was getting paranoid.  I walked into the shop only to find out about an appointment I had forgotten.  I wasn't even set up for a tattoo.  I had put the drawing in the folder for the client, and John had it sitting out on the counter.

"From the look on your face," John smiled, "You forgot about your appointment, and you forgot that I put the drawing in here to save it for you?"  I nodded to him.  He continued, "I also took the liberty of setting up your booth for the tattoo, and all you need to do is set up your machines and ink."

"Thank you, John.  Remind me to give you a raise."

"Oh, Chris, sir, I won't let you forget.  Believe me."

The tattoo was a saving grace for me.  It helped me to calm down.  By the time I finished the tattoo, it was almost midnight, almost time to go home.  We all left around twelve-thirty.  John and I went to a bar for a drink.  It wasn't until we got to the bar that it dawned on me that it was Saturday.  We are closed on Sunday and Monday, except for appointments.  The week had been busy, and I had lost track of the days as usual.  John was the one that seemed to keep things organized and running well.

"Hey, Chris.  I gotta talk to you about something," John's face had grown sad.

I was startled to see him like this, "What is it?"

"I will be straight about this.  Business is going to be short on taxes this year.  I talked to the accountant, and we did not put enough into the impound account this year.  It is my fault, and I am sorry.  The accountant and I both thought it would be enough, but we were off a bit."

"What is a bit?" Usually, I would be flipping out right now, but not with two million at my house.

"Well. Sorry, but we are going to be off by about five grand." John grins and shrugs his shoulders. "It is because we decided to cancel the advertising on the billboards. We forgot to adjust for that in the impound account."

I try to act like I usually do, "Well! What the fuck am I supposed to do now? Just shit out five grand. I mean, do you think I have that kind of cash just lying around the house? Fuck?"

"Well, Chris. You do have it lying around, and it is just not at your house. It is in a bank account, you don't remember, do you? I can tell by that look on your face."

"Wait. What? What account?"

"The account that we set up for you when we incorporated the shop five years ago! God damn it, Chris! This is the shit that irritates me."

"Woah. Calm down. So, I forgot. What is the big deal?"

"Well, nothing other than the interest that you did not pay taxes on. I guess unless the accountant figured that into your taxes, which she probably did. So, I guess no reason," John shakes his head. "You always say that you don't have any money—the reason why Chris is that you ignore your finances. You have me do it. What if I was stealing from you? How would you even know?"

A chill ran down my back. John was right. I had been here, but not here for a while.

"Well, good thing I trust you—cousin or not. I trust you. You have always taken care of things for me." I look at him across the table and try to act excited, "So, how much are we talking? Millions?"

"No. Dumbass, enough to cover the taxes, I am sure.  Not a lot more, but enough."  John looks at me like the dumbass I am.  As a kid, he always cared for me, the younger cousin.  John went to college for business.  He got me off the streets after I went druggie for a while. He convinced me to go to art school.  So, I started my graphic arts career.  I was well known and started getting into tattoos.  The next thing you know, I am begging for an apprenticeship at my friend's tattoo studio.  Fifteen years later, at the ripe age of forty-two, I am where I am now.  After twenty years at forty-two years old, John had retired from his job early.  He asked me if he could help me build my business.  I said yes.  That was five years ago when I was 37 years old.  Together we have made the tattoo shop into a thriving business.  We have six full-time artists.

We sell shirts, hats, jewelry, and other tattoo-related shit; the tattoo shop looks like a high-dollar place in Vegas.  We are on the coast of southern California.  Close enough to Los Angeles to get a high price for tattoos and plenty of clients, but far enough, it is not crazy at night.  I was still a dumb-ass kid out of art school turned tattoo artist—still painting and tattooing instead of getting that corporate art job.  John, on the other hand, was all business.  He was always the one with the head on his shoulders.  He could convince an Eskimo to buy a freezer.  I thought about telling him what happened with the money and cocaine, but I did not want him to get involved with the cartel shit.  So, I kept it to myself.

"So, can you make arrangements to take care of it, John?"

"Yes, Chris, I can," John shakes his head. "Do you ever take anything seriously?"

"Sure, I do.  I take my art seriously.  You help me by taking care of all the grown-up shit so that I can be me.  Thanks, by the way."

"Sure, Chris, sure.  Hey, Alicia and I are going to the lake with the kids.  Do you want to go?"

"Maybe.  Only if you leave me alone about being a dumbass," I smile and down my drink.

"Time to go to bed.  I will call you tomorrow.  Keep your phone on at the lake."

"Okay, I will.  See you tomorrow, I hope."

We both go our separate ways and head for home.  I pull into my house around two a.m. and go straight to bed.  I sleep like the dead.  It is the best sleep of my life, and I wake up at eight-thirty in the morning.  I take a shower and put on some shorts and a tank top. I called John and told him I would meet him at the docks.  He tells me to be there at eleven.  I take my street glide up to the lake.

John is at the docks, and I climb aboard his wakeboard boat.  It is an aluminum-hulled twenty-four-foot wakeboard boat, costing him two hundred and fifty thousand.  It has everything you could ever want on a boat and then some.

Johnny Jr. is a very good wakeboarder, and so is Tammie, John and Alicia's daughter.  Both kids are spoiled teenagers.  The kids each have a couple of friends on the boat.  Six teens and four adults.  Alicia has brought her sister Anne whom she has been trying to fix me up with for the last two years.  I hop aboard, and we cruise out of the marina for a fun-filled day full of beer and fun.  Anne and I hit it off and enjoyed the day.  According to John, she is not my type of girl, but then again, who is.  By the time we get back to the docks, I am worn out.  John has a campsite where he parked the triple axel fifth-wheel trailer with slide-outs, they are staying in for two days, and he invites me to stay the night. The trailer is massive and is the kind that is not allowed at all campsites because of its size. They call it a toy hauler. John uses it when he goes to the beach or the dunes to ride their quads and Razors.  I agree, and we stay up and drink beer while the teens are off doing their own thing.  We sit around a fire pit that John has put red and yellow LED lights in as per Alicia.  It looks cool since you can't have a fire out here in southern California.

The California weather was perfect to be out by the lake watching the stars. It was around eighty degrees, and there was a cool breeze from the wind blowing over the lake. You could hear voices, music, and even a dog barking now and then. This was the high life. I wondered why I didn't do things like this more often. We laugh, drink beer, and talk late into the morning.

We are finally all heading into the trailer to sleep. I slept on the pull-out bed on the couch, and I was kind of wishing for some company, but that never happened.

# Two

Sometimes I look back on my life and wonder where I would be without the people involved in the mix.  To say I am fortunate is an understatement.  I am sure that most people think I am untrustworthy because I am heavily tattooed from head to toe.  My head and face are tattooed, as are my hands.  My back and chest were tattooed years ago and were my first tattoos.  My upper legs are the tattoos I put on myself, trying to learn how to tattoo.  They are the worst tattoos on my body.  My lower legs and feet are quality tattoos covering my body like the rest.  I have had the luck and honor to be tattooed by some very well-known tattoo artists.  I would do anything for my family and friends.  I guess the reason why is because I do not have anyone else.  I have no brothers and sisters, and my mom and dad passed away about eighteen years ago.  I have been on my own for quite a while.  My parents left me the house and a small amount of money that John helped me pay the taxes on the house.  The only other things I have are the shop, my 1992 Chevy extended cab truck, and my 1995 Harley Street Glide.  I guess I make a good living.  I do about two hundred thousand dollars in tattooing and painting a year. Still, it is around one-hundred-fifty thousand after taxes.  Not bad for a single guy.  John puts money away to keep me in the black as he says.  He also keeps my taxes in line for me as well.  John is the driving force behind the shop's success, and he has tripled the value of the shop since I hired him five years ago.  John came in and incorporated the shop and set up the accounts that allowed me to create art and play. I drive John crazy because I am still an unruly kid with too much money. I drink too much, I am careless with my girlfriends, and I don't keep them longer than six months before breaking up with them.

It has been a week since the lake trip. John keeps asking if I have called Anne yet, and I keep saying no. It is nine in the morning, and today is the first day I have opened the safe. I take out the small package that holds twenty-three hundred. I pulled the money out of the package and put it in my wallet. The safe smells like cocaine. That crap has a smell. I decided to take a small bump of coke, so I stabbed the bundle with my pocketknife. I must poke it a couple of times to get any on the blade and what I do end up with is a small chunk. I figure that I am this far into it that I take the small chunk into the kitchen and put it on a plate. I crush it up and line it out. It ends up making a fat line. Way too big for me to do without knowing how pure it is. So, I end up dividing it into four small thin lines. I roll up a bill and snort a line. My face goes numb immediately. I realized it was the purest coke I have ever had, and I started to get a bit scared. The next thing I know, I am jamming in my truck on the way to the shop at nine-thirty in the morning. I thought my heart was going to seize up. I pulled up to the shop and spent at least five minutes trying to get my key in the front door lock. I finally got the front door open, and I walked in turned on the lights. I walked back to my booth and didn't even think about the alarm until it went off. It scared the shit out of me. I ran to the keypad and punched in the number. The phone rang as the monitoring service called to check-up. I answered and told them it was a mistake; I took too long to turn it off. I told them I was carrying in supplies and couldn't get to the keypad in time. I answered the questions, and they said the alarm was reset.

John pulled up with a weird look on his face. "Chris, what are you doing here?" He asks me as he gets out of his Escalade. "Are you okay? You look a little pale and sweaty. You have a heart attack or something?"

"No, why?" All I think is I am caught. Fuck, fuck, fuck. All I can think is, why did I do that line? "I am just doing some cleaning to my booth. Can't I clean my booth?" I am all irritated that John is questioning me at MY tattoo shop.

"Okay. Hang on, turbo. Why are you getting angry? Slow your roll. It is just that the last time I saw you here this early was when the county was coming in to regulate the industry for the first time."

"Sorry. I am just a little edgy," I know that John can tell I am high as fuck right now. I can't help but wipe my nose, "I didn't sleep well last night."

"Chris? Did you do some coke?"

"Me? No, why do you ask?"

"Cause there is white shit on your nose, duh."

"Oh." Caught. God damn it. I can't seem to do anything right. "Yeah, well, sorry, dad."

"Dude. I don't care if you do that once in a while, and just don't go out driving in this condition. You are high as fuck and still have white all over your face."

John and I mop the shop and do a deep cleaning. I take out all the garbage and start washing the windows, and John comes out laughing at me.

"Man, you need to do that shit more often. You are a little miss

Merry Maid on that shit." He laughs and pats me on the shoulder. "Did you meet some little coke whore last night?"

"Uh. Yeah. Sorry just got caught up in the moment." I laugh and go back into the shop. The clock has to be wrong. It has only been an hour since I snorted the line. No wonder John thinks I am all wound up. Because I am all wound up. I shook my head and laughed, and walked into the shop. I go to my booth and start drawing. I am trying to clear my head. I started thinking about that coke on the plate back at my house. That shit is the best I have ever had. It must be pure and never cut. I wonder how much it is worth. I don't know anyone that would know about drug prices and how much a kilo of pure cocaine would be. I am too paranoid about looking it up on the computer. I start looking for drug programs on the shop TV and found a couple. I watch the program about the drug cops on the border. They seem to think it is about twenty-five thousand a kilo. So, it must be close to that, I figure. That means I have around fifty thousand dollars of cocaine at my house in my safe. I don't even know what to do with all of it.

I figure I will leave it in the safe for now, except for the lines on the plate at home. I figure I could make double the lines with what is on the plate. It is strong. Later in the morning, around eleven am, a cop comes in to ask questions. Did anyone see anything? Did anyone find anything around the property? When the cop leaves, I realize it is not a real cop car. The cartel members are brazen enough to ask questions about what happened to the money the cops did not find.

Three more bodies were found in the county a couple of days later. One of the bodies turns out to be a cop. The officer's burned-up car is found on a dirt road, and the officer is in the car. The funny thing is the officer's head is in the back seat. The other bodies are said to be local drug dealers.  They, too, had their heads removed.  The news states that anytime drugs and money go missing, you must expect dead bodies to follow up.  I am glad that I kept the money and drugs in my safe.  I am not taking a chance of getting caught with any of it.  I figured that I would use a little of the money at a time, and no one would notice.  As for the drugs, I think I will stay away from them for a while, but I will keep them in the safe as well.  I know I can stay away from it.  John may not think I can because I had to go to rehab three different times, but I can do it.  He would flip his lid if he found out I had two kilos of pure cocaine in my safe, not to mention two and a half million in my safe.  Suddenly, I remembered Corky Romano's movie where he got high on coke and started yelling, he should buy a boat. I started laughing because I could buy a boat right now.  John walked into my booth to tell me the county was there, and they wanted to talk to me too.

"I should buy a boat!" I blurted out and laughed like an idiot.

"Try not to act like an addict right now, please?"  He shook his head and walked back to the front of the shop.

I am too mad to say anything as I walk past John to greet the county inspector.  When the county inspector leaves, I realize that we will have to spend more money on the shop.  They now want pedals at each sink, so it is hands-free.  I also must have a hands-free soap dispenser, hand sanitizer, and a hands-free towel dispenser at each tattoo station.  It won't be that big of a deal, but it is still a grip of cash.

John tells me, "Don't worry your pretty little head about it, Chris.  I got this, and I will make a call and have this finished by this week."  He turns to walk away.

"I can do shit, man. I will do this! I snapped at him. He has touched a nerve with that remark of his, and it makes me feel like a kid again.

"Sober up," John remarks, "and when you are sober. Come talk to me."

"Fuck you, John. This is my shop. Fuck you," I don't know why I am so angry right now, but I am pissed. My fists are clenched, and I am shaking. John turns and goes to his office. As he walks away, I get angrier. I went back to my booth. It is not even noon yet. It is only eleven-thirty in the morning. We don't even open for another thirty minutes. The other artists will be arriving any minute. I have a horrible headache. I decided I was going to go home. I look at my schedule and delight in the fact that I have no appointments.

I walk up front to John's office, "Hey, I have no appointments, so I am just going to go home and get out of your hair. Sorry for this morning."

"That is no good. Everyone is booked out, and you are the only one that can take walk-ins. Sorry, but I have to ask you to stay." John turns to look me in the eye, "Hope you make a note of the way you feel right now. We don't want to go down this road again, buddy. Tighten shit up, okay?" John turns back around to finish what he is working on.

"Uh. Yeah, okay, I guess," I don't even know how to respond to what John just did to me.

"Here, take one of these," John tosses me a bottle of pain pills, "Take one. Go get a large bottle of orange juice and something to eat."

"Thanks, John, again I am sorry, man. I am. It was just an out-of-the-blue thing, man." I want to tell him about the coke sitting in my safe, but I realize that now would be the worst possible time to tell him about it. I take one pill for my headache, and I head to the store to get something to eat and drink. Gary is at the store this morning, and I had forgotten that he was on the morning shift now.  His face brightens up when I walk into the store.

"Hey, you, mudda facka, you, where you been," he yells at me as I walk to go get orange juice and a burrito.

"Sup, Gary," I place my stuff on the counter. "Where have you been?  I have been at the shop doing what I do."

"So, were you there the night the truck crashed on the corner?"

"I was at the shop. Were you here?" I look at Gary.

"No man, I am on days now.  We have a new girl that handles my old shift," Gary winks at me.

"You dirty dog.  You finally found a sucker to take your place?"  I laugh and pay for my stuff.

"You should come in here more often, you sonna, bitch you." I laugh because Gary can't curse for shit.  He is a cool dude from New York.  He speaks Spanish fluently and broken English, and I think he is from India.

"Thanks, Gary," I walk out, and he waves back.  As I walk to the corner, Gary says, "Come back soon, you, mudda fackaaaa," over the speakers on the gas pumps.  The people pumping gas kind of jump back a little.  That is Gary for you.  He doesn't give a fuck about anything.  He is just doing Gary.  Believe it or not, Gary is married with a kid.  He manages the store.  His family owns it together.  They seem to do everything together.  The light changes and I cross to go to the shop.  The hydrant at the corner is a fresh yellow.  I cross the street and go around the canal and across the parking lot to the shop.  There are more cars and motorcycles in the lot already.  People are out front smoking and laughing.

"God damn Chris, is the world ending?  You are here early."  Susan jokes at me as I walk

by.

"I was here before you this morning Suzy-Q," I wink at her as I walk into the shop.

The shop is already bustling with business.  I go to my booth and get my station

prepared-- I get a walk-in. I finish up and go into the break room and eat and drink my

hangover cure.  My head feels better.  I forgot how bad coming down could be on coke.

The high was short and fantastic, but damn, coming off, it sucked ass.  My heart was still

kind of racing a bit.  I had forgotten about that part of the drug as well.  It was just one

line of pure coke.  Just one line, I kept telling myself that if I did that just occasionally, I

would be okay.  I wouldn't be spending money on it like before.  I could see how I got

caught up on it before.  I must get rid of that shit soon.  John comes over to the intercom

to inform me that I have a customer already.  I clean up and wash my hands.  I go up to

the front to see my new project.  It is easy enough.  It is a heart with a name on a banner

over it or through it because they can't decide.  Could I please draw up both versions?  I

draw up a heart on one sheet of paper and then draw up a couple of banners with their

names on tracing paper.  I lay the banners over the heart drawing and let them decide

what they want.

"Look, sweetheart, you can put the banners anywhere you want. How smart," the

customer looks at his wife for approval.

"That is a smart idea.  Now can you draw the banner on the heart?  One over the heart

and the other through the heart like this?"  The wife holds the banner over the drawing

to show me how she wants me to redraw it for her.

"Sorry, miss, I will draw your choice when I make the stencil, but I am not going to draw one of each for no reason." I smile and pull the drawing back to me.

"Can I take a picture and show my sister?" She brings out her phone.

"No pictures of the drawings or the art on the walls, miss," I point to the giant sign on each wall of the waiting area. I get this routine at least once a week from newbies that come in price shopping for tattoos. You draw the tattoo design, and then they take a picture of the design and go price shopping. I try to explain, "Look, miss, I usually take a deposit to draw anything. I did this for you on the spot. The tattoo will be three hundred dollars and will take about half an hour to an hour to do. You can pay John when you fill out the paperwork. Thank you, I will be getting my booth set up for you." I take the drawing and head back to my booth, irritated. John came back to my booth to tell me they would go and have lunch and decide, but they said they would be back. We both laughed about it. The rest of my day went okay. I had one customer tattoo a koi fish on his shoulder. Other than that, I just stayed in my booth.

At midnight John asks me if I want to grab something to eat. I beg off and just go home. I can see that John is worried about me. I wave goodbye and go to the house. The streets are quiet, and there is little traffic on the way home. As I pulled into the garage, the lights of the truck swung over my motorcycle. It is a nice bike, but it could use some TLC. My mind races about what I could do to it now. Maybe a new front wheel and extended bags! A new paint job? New exhaust. I could do these things—my mind races as I think about the possibilities.

I could finally have that bagger I always wanted. It should be straightforward. I would pay cash as I go and get it done on the low low. I turn on my iPad and start looking at wheelsets. I found a set of wheels that looked dope. I found a package deal on a twenty-six-inch front wheel and an eighteen-inch back wheel. Both were big diamond spoke wheels. The wheels and tires were six thousand. The extended bags were three thousand with LED lights and back fender. I was excited. I would call in the morning. I finally went to bed around three in the morning.

I woke up to my phone ringing. I looked at the clock. It was noon. Shit. I was going to be late again. I jumped in the shower. A quick once around my body, my hair, brushed my teeth, didn't shave. I got out of the shower and got dressed. I started out the door when the phone rang again. It was John. Damn it.

"Hey. John, I am on my way," I answered quickly to head him off.

"Listen, Chris. The shop was broken into last night. Get here as soon as you can," He hung up. John did not sound worried. Weird.

My heart seemed to freeze up. What if it was the cartel trying to find out if I was the one that took their stuff? I hurried downstairs and got in my truck, and headed out. The drive over to the shop seemed to take forever. I hit every traffic light and got behind every slow person in the world. It was like these people were on permanent vacation or something. They were all out to slow me down. Finally, I could see the shop with a parking lot full of cop cars. They were out front and on the side of the shop at the secondary door. That is weird because that door only has two bolt locks and no handle on the outside of the door. No one has ever tried to get in through that door. Maybe they went out that door. I pulled into the lot and parked. John rushed over to meet me.

"Good, you're sober. Right?" John looked me in the eyes.

"Yes," I said, irritated as hell.

John continues, "Well, there are cops everywhere. So anyway, they broke in through the front door and went out through the back door. Kind of weird that they would go that route, but whatever. They did not take much."

"Didn't take much? That is too weird," my head is spinning again.

"Yeah. The cops said they broke into all of these buildings in our complex last night. Must have been multiple people," John looked like a kid watching a Superman movie.

"Who do they think it was?" I asked.

"Well, the cops seemed to think that it was the cartel trying to find out if anyone from this area took their stuff. Or maybe their stuff was hidden around here somewhere, scary, huh?" John did not seem to be bothered by this very much.

"What did they take?" I was pissed now. Not so much scared anymore when I realized they were just taking a shot in the dark. There would be no evidence of anything at the shop. I suddenly thought of my house. Oh, shit. If they went to my house, they would find the safe and their stuff. I had to get that shit out of there. Now I started to get nervous.

"The thieves took the cash register and our small safe. They were empty, so no big deal. The robbers left everyone's tattoo stuff alone, thank God. They took a couple of books and a computer".

"Which computer?" I wanted to know.

"The shop computer in the drawing area. That is going to be expensive to replace," John seemed to be upset at that. "Come on, and let's go talk to the police." John led the way.

The day was shot. The cops seemed to be everywhere as they investigated the whole complex of eight businesses. Each business had been broken into, and the stuff taken was primarily computers and registers and safes. We seemed to have gotten off easy for the most part because we had insurance to cover most of the stuff that was stolen. The doors were fixed by that afternoon. John had called the computer place that did all our work to discover all the programs we used. Most of the stuff was on a stashed server in the storage room, locked in a cabinet. The computer that was taken was an Apple computer with a twenty-seven-inch screen. It was costly and had all the graphics programs you can imagine. At least the robbers did not take the cloud server with all the drawings and graphics work on it. We would have to replace the computer and several programs, but that was all. John had almost everything lined up with the insurance company before five that evening.

The cops interviewed every one of us. The artists were pissed because of missed appointments and not being able to access the computer for work, but other than that, it was not as bad as I thought it would be. I had called that afternoon, and I had gotten a storage locker at the local storage place to store my loot. I left the shop around six and went straight home to gather up all the money and dope, load it in my truck, and put it in the storage locker. I went back home and went to bed early. The thoughts and dreams about my motorcycle were gone, and I felt like I was a prisoner on the run. I got up early the following day, took a shower, and went to get breakfast. After breakfast, I went to the local bookstore to browse around and see if I could find something interesting to read.

I found a book on Masonic symbols and art. It looked cool. I also found another book on sacred geometry to add to my growing collection on the subject. Afterward, I went to the art store and bought some red pencils, my favorite to draw with. I got some Bristol paper and some other things.  I got to the shop at eleven in the morning.  It is time I am supposed to be there, but I am rarely there at that time of the morning.  John and Susan were there already getting things put back in order.  The new computer was there already.  John was unpacking things while Susan put things together and set them up.  Susan had found our software discs for all the software, so we didn't have to order new software.  By noon Susan had the computer up and running.  It was a better computer than the last one we had.  Susan even had all our iPad Pros synced up and ready to go.  Most of us used Procreate anyway on our I-Pads for drawing art and printing stencils.  John said the shop came out ahead a little, so according to John, we made two hundred dollars by being robbed. The landlord had replaced all the broken doors and locks on the whole complex.  He had also hired a security company to patrol the complex again.  We had a security company when we first opened, but the landlord had let them go and had never replaced them.  That is how John had supposedly gotten the landlord to fix things.  So, all we had to do was repurchase stolen stuff.  John came back to my booth and asked if I wanted to go to lunch with him, Susan, and Troy.  I agreed, and we all went to the local pizza place to have lunch.  We all piled into John's Escalade, and off we went.  Susan started asking me right away about what I was thinking about getting high the other day.  John must have told her.

"I mean God damn it, Chris," Susan stared at me, "We just got you sober last year!  The last thing we need is for you to go on another binge."

"Yeah. I know," I am irritated.  "It was a spur of the moment thing.  I know those are the worst kinds.  I am good, I swear."  I crossed my heart with my middle finger.

"Always playing around," Susan sneered at me, "I swear to God, I am not going to stick around to watch you do this shit again."

I realized John had pulled together an intervention, not a lunch, "Look, guys, I swear to God. I will give you my motorcycle if I start this shit again."

The pizza arrived just in time. Troy just looked at me and nodded. He knew what was up. He had gone through the same shit, and he helped me get clean. I had to get that shit out of my house. The sooner, the better. I just had to think of who to sell it to. I had not thought about the tricky business of trying to sell that much cocaine, pure cocaine. I took the stuff to storage. I guess I thought I would just use a little of it here and there. That idea was an addict's idea. That idea would get me spun out again, and I would probably end up dead. I am a grade A dumb ass when I get high.

"Chris to Earth," John was snapping his fingers.

"Huh," I laughed nervously, "Sorry, I was thinking about something."

"You sure you're sober?" Susan squinted at me.

"Yeah, I am sure. Test me!" I regretted that as soon as I said it.

"Nah, it would just come up dirty," Troy said with a mouthful of pizza. "Maybe next week, and it will be out of your system by then." He winked at me and kept eating.

I didn't know if I should kick him under the table or not. We finished eating pizza and had a couple of beers. We all had appointments today. These people here at the table had been with me throughout many years, dark years, happy years, successful years, and failing years. They had all stayed my friends, no, not friends, family. They had stayed with me through all the stupid shit. Susan and Troy worked with me at several tattoo places before starting the tattoo shop. John had come in after I had screwed shit up. He came in and made everything right.  I owed a lot to these people.  I could not let them down.  I had to get rid of the cocaine, and soon.

The shop was busy as hell when we got back, and everyone was in a bitchy mood because John wasn't there to hold their hand and do their paperwork for them.  All the money and paperwork lay in a pile on the front desk.

"See Chris. This is why we need to hire a receptionist.  This shit right here," John pointed at the mountain of paperwork and money. "Is this stuff split already," John said out loud so the others could hear.

They all answered different answers.  So, John had to take the paperwork and cash to each booth to see what belonged where.  Now they were all irritated.

"I swear to God it is like babysitting," John spoke out loud to no one in particular.

I shake my head, "Then hire someone.  You always say this shit, but you never do it.  Hire someone, God damn it," I wait for his answer, "I know. Hire Anne.  Does she have a job now? Hire her."  I walk off and go to my booth to set up my appointment. "Yeah, John, hire Anne so Chris's can actually get a piece of ass," Susan laughed as she walked into her booth.

"Fuck you, Susan," I yelled across the shop.

The shop erupted into a cacophony of chimpanzee noises.

John hated us doing this shit, which is why we did it even more.

Troy started yelling at me, "Hey. What's your name?"

I answered, "Tony."

"Well, fuck you, Tony," Troy answered.

"What's your name?" I shot back.

"Ezekiel," Troy answered back.

"Well, fuck you, Ezekiel," everyone yelled and laughed. We did this whole thing that we watched on social media, and it makes John angry when we do it. But we had to finish the whole routine. Now, everyone was yelling it. "Fuck you, Ezekiel."

"You know what I did last night."

"You better not bring my mom into this."

"I built a fire by the river."

"Oh."

"And then I fucked your mom by it."

John walked into the office and slammed the door. We all burst out laughing, and he is lucky we are not acting like Dori talking to whales or continuing to scream like chimpanzees. It can get worse around here.

Tattoo machines buzzed, and clients and artists laughed and joked as they did the tattoos. It was what tattooing was all about. The whole experience. The connection of being cool and hanging out with cool people. That is why I have never gone into a corporate job. I got to hang out with really cool people, create really cool art and put it on really cool people. AND then get paid to do it. Now, how cool is that?

# Three

It has been three weeks since our lunch date slash intervention.  John hired a new artist, Mikail or Mick.  He is from Russia, and he has an excellent reputation.  We met him at the Amsterdam tattoo convention.  He is here for who knows how long, guest spot, or permanent.  John also listened to me and hired Anne.  She started a week ago, and she has been too busy training to talk to me, or John told her to stay away from me.  I have been tattooed at a convention since the lunch date.  I went to Long Beach and tattooed on the Queen Mary at the Ink and Iron convention.  I got to see a lot of my friends.  I stayed busy the whole convention and made a bit of money.  I had broken even on the cost of the convention by five o'clock the first day.

All the rest was cake, as they say.  I got to visit, drink, and hang out with other tattoo artists.  I took some extra cash and bought a rotary tattoo machine that made me tattoo slower. It took me a little longer than average for the piece I tattooed, but the client was none the wiser.  The tattoo was so smooth and crisp.  I fell in love with this machine immediately.

Anyway, I have been back at the shop for a week and a half.  It is four o'clock Wednesday, and I am booked out.  I got here at the shop at noon and started tattooing right away.  I just finished, and my next tattoo is waiting.  I am behind.  My next tattoo is going to be at least six hours.  John was kind enough to get me a hamburger and a coke.

I set up my booth and went into the break room to eat.  I will be ready to tattoo by five,

and I should be finished by eleven.  I hope I am finished by eleven.

The break room is quiet and deserted, and the shop is loud and crowded.  It is nice to sit

down and eat, and I usually do not sit down and eat when we are this busy.  I am about

halfway through my hamburger when Anne walks into the room, and I put my burger

down, expecting to have to go back to work.

"Hey, Chris, why don't you talk to me," Anne asks me straight up.  "I thought we hit it off

okay at the lake."

Wow, I did not see that coming, "Huh?  What do you mean?"

"Well, no call, not two words since I got here, that is what I mean," She sits down

opposite of me.

"I was giving you some space.  I didn't realize that you were interested?" Man, I did not

see this at all.  She is a gorgeous girl.

"Oh," she looks at me for a minute, "So, do you want to go get a drink tonight when you

are finished or what?"

"Or what.  But a drink is cool too," I smile and wink.

"Is or what, going to be at your house or mine?"  She twists her hair and stares at me.

"Uh, my house?" Now I am bewildered.  Did I just make a date for her to spend the

night?  Did I just get lucky?

"Good. I will leave you alone now."  She gets up and goes back to work.

My appointment is waiting, so I finish my lunch and return to my booth.  When I get to

my booth, I pour the ink and get out my skin pens, ink pens that write on the skin.  Anne

comes back and asks if I am ready for the client to return.  I nod my head, yes, and she goes out and brings my client back to me.  The artwork is a back piece, stencil, and partly

drawn with an ink pen.  I am only doing the outline of the tattoo today.  It takes me at

least an hour to get the design drawn on before even starting to tattoo.  I spray some

sealer over the ink pen to keep it from smearing and wiping off.  It is six-thirty by the

time I start tattooing.  I look up at the clock and to my surprise it twelve-thirty.  I look at

the tattoo and calculate about one hour more of tattoo time.  I start to get bummed out

because I am thinking of no date.

"Hey, Chris," John pokes his head around the corner. "Are you finished yet?"

I fight back my sarcastic response, "About an hour, John, why?"

"Joe still needs to pay.  You want me to take care of it now before I close out?"

"Here is my credit card John," Joe pulls his credit card from his shirt pocket.

"That will work. Don't move, Joe."  I start tattooing again.  John leaves and comes back

with the paperwork for Joe to sign.

"See you tomorrow, Chris," John turns, speaking as he goes, "I will lock up on my way

out."

I keep tattooing.  I finish and look up at the clock, and it is two in the morning.  Damn it, I

hate being wrong, and I was way off.

"All done, Joe, you know the routine.  Call me if you have any questions.  I have you on

the calendar in three weeks. Is that cool?"

"That will work.  I will see you then, man."

I unlock the door and let Joe out.  I start back to my booth to clean up.  As I walk into my

booth, I see someone in my booth cleaning up.  It is Anne, and she scares the living shit

out of me.  I must have screamed like a girl because I scare her too.

"What the fuck, you scream like a little girl," she starts laughing.

"I didn't know you were still here.  I thought I was here by myself," I am laughing like an idiot.  "So, does this mean I am going to get laid?"

"Don't get in a hurry, buddy," she winks at me, "You gotta show me more than that?"

I jump in on the cleaning, and the next thing you know, she is following me to my house. I fix us some pizza rolls and grab some beers.  We sit on the couch and start watching a movie while we sit and talk to each other.  We snuggle up together on the couch and start kissing.  Now, I am not one for kissing and telling, but we did not get any sleep that night, and we took a shower together in the morning.

"Hey, Chris, I have to get home and change clothes," she kisses me and starts to get dressed.

"Hey, what about breakfast?"

"Nope. I have to be at work before you get there. You know, before you, Chris."

"Why?"

"You know why smart-ass," she smirks and cocks her head with her hands on her hips.

"Are you afraid of John?"

"NO. I am afraid of Alicia, my sister."

"Oh, yeah. Right." I had forgotten about her. "I thought she was trying to hook us up?"

"Yeah, but not for me to put out on the first date."

"I am not going to say anything to her," I slap her on the butt.

"Slow your roll there, mister.  There will be none of this shit at the shop. Understood?"

"No problem, I am not afraid of John or his wife, Alicia."  I smile and turn to go get dressed.

"Well, I will see you at work. Be a little late today."

"That is easy for me. See you at the shop around one-thirty."

I watch her walk out to her ninety-three Honda Acura. It is a flat black piece of crap with red stock rims. The car sounds like it is going a million miles an hour as it creeps down the road. It is a typical street racing car. She must have bought that piece of crap off some kid. I go back into the house and lock the door. I set my alarm clock and lay down to go to sleep. My alarm goes off at noon. I get up. I wash my face, brush my teeth, and comb my hair. The ride to work went faster than usual, so I kept going down the street to Jack in the Box. I get a Jumbo Jack and a Coke. By the time I get to the shop, it is two in the afternoon. My buddy Frank is here to talk about working on my bagger.

We might trade out some work. Frank follows me to my booth, where we negotiate the plans for my bagger. Twenty-six-inch front wheel and an eighteen-inch rear wheel. I want extended jumbo bags with an air-ride system. And last of all a high-powered stereo system. The price for parts alone came out to twenty thousand, and the labor would be a straight trade across for a back piece. I had to pay for the parts upfront, so I decided to pick up the cash. Frank and I walk upfront, telling John that I have to go to the bank. I go to the storage place, grab the cash, and then drive directly to Frank's shop to pay for my parts. Frank will pick up my bike at the house and start on the neck of the frame. I get my ass back to the shop.

I am late for my appointment. John gives them a one-hundred-dollar discount because I am late, that fucker, anyway, I get right on it. It is a koi fish tattoo on a young chick's thigh. Easy peasy. It is a seven-hour tattoo, at the least. Anne acts like she doesn't even know me. John tells her to go get food for the crew, so she goes to the taco truck and gets four tacos per person, along with cokes.  Anne comes to tell me there is food and I

should eat.  I spray some lidocaine on my client's tattoo, and we take a food break.  We

go and eat in the break room.  Anne sits at the other end of the table with Troy and

Susan.  My client Rachel flirts with me over our tacos.  It is a common thing to happen,

actually.  I watch Anne's reaction, but no reaction.  We finished our tacos and cokes.

I finish the tattoo around fifteen after ten.  I have no more appointments, so I begin

cleaning up my booth.  I find the ritual of tattooing exciting.  The drawing and creating of

art for people to wear for life.  The actual laser focus during the tattooing process and

the actual loss of self during the tattoo process.  It is very relaxing for me.  It seems to

swallow me up.  It is better than most drugs because it makes time go by; it makes hours

seem like minutes.  The clean-up process seems to bring things to a close for me, and it is

very much part of that process for me.  As I cleaned up my booth, Rachel left me her

number with a note.  That number goes right into the top drawer of my tool cabinet.

Anne popped into my booth and asked if I would like to meet up again.  I agree, and we

have decided to meet at my house at eleven-thirty tonight.  She is off work now, so she

leaves.

I go up front to hang out with the shop crew for a while.  We decide to go to the next

convention in Las Vegas and maybe Reno just for fun.  We all need to take a work

vacation.  Go someplace to work hard, play harder.  The phone rings, and John answers; I

can tell it is all bad because John starts to shake his head.  John hangs up the phone.

"Well, sorry to say this, but Susan got in a wreck on her way home.  She will be okay, but

they think she broke her back," John breaks down crying.

"What hospital?" John, Susan, and I are like family, and it hits us hard.

John calls the whole crew, including Alicia and Anne.  We all meet at the hospital to go

see Susan.  They let us look through the window in the ICU, but no one can go visit her

yet.  We all camp out in the waiting room, taking pictures and dicking around. The

security guard tells us all to go home, but we stay and settle in for a long night.  We all

crash out on the couches and sleep and wait.  The hospital staff comes by around seven-

thirty in the morning to let us know that she is awake.  We can wave at her from the

window, but we cannot go in yet.  When we go to the ICU, the nurse lets John see Susan.

The rest of us wave at her from the window.  John comes out teary-eyed and asks if we

want to close the shop today to stay close and come back and visit Susan.  The guys say

they will go to the shop and hold down the fort.  Anne says she is going to go in and help

too.  John and I talk about it, and we decide to take shifts at the hospital until Susan is

out of the ICU.  John takes the first shift, and he stays as the rest of us take off.  Anne

calls me to let me know she is on the way to my house.  I am beaten, but I agree to meet

her at my place.  Anne and I end up snuggling up together in my bed and fall asleep until

John calls and wakes us up.  Susan has been downgraded to severe and is scheduled to

go to surgery and told me to stay home.  John and Alicia are going home to rest.  I hung

up the phone and told Anne.  We end up going back to sleep for another couple of hours.

I called the shop to let them know what was up with Susan.  The shop was closed.  No

one answered the phone.  I guess they all were as tired as Anne and I were.  Anne and I

ventured out for some Italian food and then returned to the house.  We spent the rest of

the day and night in each other's arms.

Anne and I went to the hospital the following day and brought flowers and balloons for

Susan.  When we get up to ICU, they tell us that no balloons or flowers are allowed in

ICU.  Susan is still in surgery.  Anne and I go to get some breakfast in the hospital cafeteria. We meet John and Alicia as they are coming in to see Susan.  We tell them the skinny on Susan, and we all go and get breakfast together.

"So, Chris, you like Anne, huh," Alicia is smiling at me, "I told you that you two would hit it off."

"What? What are you talking about?" I am so caught off guard.  It is so awkward right now.

"Oh, I can tell you two hooked up.  John might not be able to see it, but I can see it," mischief glitters in her eyes, "When did you two start having sex?"

"Whoa, wait now. Who said that?  Not me?" I am desperately waiting for help from Anne.

"Oh, Chris, the secret is out," Anne starts laughing, "Women can tell. Duh."  Anne starts laughing and turns to Alicia, "I hunted him down scored on the first night, and we have been seeing each other for a while now."

"Oh, I could tell. You are one aggressive girl." Alicia and Anne start jabbering to each other like I am not there.

John looks at me and shakes his head, "You know Alicia is going to kill you if you break her heart."  He starts laughing at me.

I just sit there with my face feeling all hot and embarrassed.  I have never felt like this; I usually embarrass other people.  I sit quietly at the table and try to tune out the women. I try to eat in silence.  John brings up the issue of Susan and her being out of work.  I get this bright idea about paying off her mortgage for a year.  I have a mountain of cash, and I could do it without anyone knowing about it.

"Chris. Earth to Chris," John is snapping his fingers in my face, and now everyone is looking at me.

"Huh?" My face flushes, "Sorry, I was thinking about Susan."

"About that. I think that we could find the money to help Susan out. We could do a fundraiser for her at the shop. She has a ton of clients, and I am sure that they would all donate for her," John smiles and stares at me.

"Well, that is what I was thinking about. We could just pay Suzan's mortgage ahead," I look at Alicia and Anne, and they smile at me.

"Well yeah, but who is going to take care of her? She has no one to take care of her," Alicia's eyes are glistening with tears, "She has no family to help her."

"Wow. I hadn't thought of that," My mind spins at the new idea.

"Well, maybe we could have her at our house?" Alicia looks at John with puppy dog eyes.

"Well, I guess," John shrugs, "We have an extra room. I am sure that the other driver's insurance will take care of some of her care."

"What about her house?" I am feeling frustrated.

"Well, we could store all of her stuff, I guess, until she is back on her feet," John says this like it is the only choice.

"You think she will lose her house?" I ask tentatively.

"Call Sam, your friend that is the lawyer," Alicia is focused.

"I had not thought about that; I guess I could," I take out my phone. While I am on the phone with Sam, the others are hashing out details for Susan.

We finish up breakfast and head up to the surgery waiting room. Sam will get things straightened out for Susan and get back to me. He told me not to worry because he would make sure that she came out great in the end.  We walk into the waiting room, go to the desk, and ask if Susan is out of surgery.  We were told that they could not release patient information to non-family members.  John went into the manager's office.  He was gone for a very long time.  When he returned, he had good news.  Susan would be out of recovery in an hour, and she would be back in ICU where she would stay for two more days, and then it would be out to a regular room.  John said the doctor said the surgery went well and that she should be back at work in about six months.  Susan would be just fine. We all sighed a collective sigh of relief.  Now we had to work out the bills issue and her housing issue.  Other than that, everything would be okay.

# Four

It has been six weeks since Susan's wreck. She has been living in her own house. Sam got the insurance company to pick up the medical and Susan's expenses. As for the house, I worked out something with Sam to take care of the housing issue. Susan owed one hundred thousand on her house, and he said that she would pay it off with the settlement she would get from the wreck. So, I got the money for Sam to pay off the house in the meantime. Sam said he would figure out a way to get it back to me, and he set it up like a loan. He sold the idea to Susan as an installment to take care of her house until the settlement came in. Susan was able to take care of herself.

The doctors had fused two vertebrae right between the shoulders. According to the doctors, she was stiff, but she should be okay to tattoo. We all know that doctors are morons for the most part. They mean they practice in their practice. Susan and I would go to physical therapy together. I went to help her as she helped me when I was going to rehab. We have history, and some of that history is pretty dark. Susan and John have history too. They dated back when we were all kids. Susan and I had just graduated from high school, and I introduced her to John. They hit it off, and they dated for about a year. Susan kicked John to the curb when he was going to college. John went to work in the business industry and high finance. Susan and I did the art path of life. Susan and I started tattooing around the age of eighteen. I would not trade those years for anything.

Susan was like a sister to me.  She was young when her mom died in a car crash.  Susan's dad died about three years ago.  It has been hard on her, and she does not have any family around this area.  I don't think she has seen any family since her dad's funeral.  She had gotten her dad's house after he passed.  The bank allowed her to continue the payments on the house.  Now the house would be her's forever.  I made sure that she would not find out.  Sam would take care of all that stuff for me.

Mick, the guy from Russia, had stepped up and worked in Susan's place.  All her clients had said they would wait, but the walk-in clients still needed to be handled.   The shop kept running smoothly even without Susan.  Everyone knows about Anne and me, and she stays with me around two to three times a week.  I started tattooing Frank's back last week in trade for the work on my bagger; the tattoo is a Frank Frazzetta piece called The Death Dealer, very sick. He was ready for his next appointment and would be here Friday, three days from now.  John still does not know about the cash or my motorcycle, for that matter.  We went to the lake every Sunday for the last four weeks.  Anne and I had gotten close, and we had talked about her maybe moving in next month.  The only reason we had not moved in together yet is that Susan had told me to wait.  She said I needed to make sure that she wasn't out for my money and stuff.  I honestly had never thought about it in that light until Susan had said something.  Anne seemed to be a little jealous of Susan and me spending so much time together.  John had even told Anne that Susan and I went back to middle school and were like family.

Frank came in for his tattoo and informed me that my bike was finished, and he was having someone bring it over.  I will be taking it out tomorrow, Saturday, for a ride.

"Chris, come up front," it was John over my intercom.

"On my way," I responded over the intercom.

Frank winked at me, and I tore off my gloves. I feel like a kid at Christmas. I rush upfront, and Frank's mechanic, Pedro, is there in the front. Pedro was dangling my keys from his hand. I barrel out the front door. There, parked on the sidewalk in front of the shop, is my baby. My bike is all gloss black. No decals, nothing. The motor is chromed out, and the exhaust is chromed out fishtails, but the rest of the bike is gloss black. The big front wheel goes all the way up to the bottom of the front fairing. The stretched jumbo bags almost touch the ground, and the leather seat has a tattoo machine. The yellow-brown seat looks excellent on the gloss black bike. The lids of the bags have two speakers each. The front fairing has oversize speakers as well. It looks B-A-D-A-S-S, and it is mine.

Everyone is jabbering about how badass the bike looks.

"Chris, start it up and go for a ride," Pedro pushes me towards the bike.

"Go on, Chris, it won't bite you," Frank laughs at me.

I start it up, and it feels like a new bike, almost foreign to me. It sounds great. The stereo is super loud, and everyone holds their ears. Pedro shows me where the air-ride switch is located. I raise the bike and take off out of the parking lot. I didn't stay gone long—just about five minutes at the most. When I come back, there is no one out front.

"Well, Chris. You like the bike?" Pedro pats me on the shoulder when I walk into the shop.

"Is the Pope Catholic?" I hug Pedro, and I high-five Frank. "Holy fuck, that bike looks badass."

"God damn Chris, where did you find the cash to do that?" John asks.

"Dude, I have been saving up for this forever." I am lying out my ass, and John should know that I can't save money to save my life. I make a lot, but I cannot save a penny.

"That is the best-looking bike in the area," Troy boasts. "We gotta take it out tonight."

"Hell yeah. Where are we going?" I ask.

"Let's go to Santa Monica to the pier," Troy suggests.

"I am there. Anne, you want to go to the pier tonight?" I look at Anne.

"I am there already," She walks over and hugs me. "I would follow you anywhere."

We all filter back to work. Frank and I chop it up as I tattoo him. I finish him up at eleven. Troy and Anne are waiting for me. Anne will follow me to the house to drop off the truck, and we will meet Troy at his house on our way out towards the pier. We get to the house and pick up a helmet for Anne. We grab a jacket and head on out to Troy's house. Troy is waiting out front sitting on his bike. When I roll around the corner, I hear Troy start his bike. I slow down as we roll up to his house, and he pulls out behind us. We roar out into the night and get on highway one and head down towards the pier. By midnight we are hitting the bars on the pier. We get home by three in the morning. I crash hard, and I don't wake up until the morning around ten. Anne shakes me awake and brings me some coffee in bed.

Anne lays down next to me and snuggles up to me as she whispers, "I had a lot of fun last night, thank you."

"Anytime. I had a lot of fun too. I love the way the bike rides; it is so smooth," I put my arm around her and squeezed.

"Chris, do you think we could take the day off? Please?" She even bats her eyes.

"I guess so. I wanted to take it out on a ride today, but you better call John to see if you can get the day off," I shrug my shoulders.

Anne calls John, "Yup, un huh, yup. Sure, I guess okay. Yes, at four this afternoon. Ok. See you later.

"Well, what was that all about Anne?"

"John says you have an appointment and that I am a company slave." So, no day off, Chris, and you have an appointment with some guy from the county."

"Oh! Oh shit. I forgot about that guy. Shit, I got to do his drawing still. Fuck." I jump up and grab my backpack and start rummaging through it to try and find the resource material for his tattoo. I get everything together and start drawing. Anne is getting to see the distracted side of me. Sometimes I lag on drawings and don't do them until the day of their appointment. Thank God it was a straightforward design, to begin with. So, I take out a shipping tube that I use to store drawings and put it in my backpack.

"Oh my God, Chris," Anne comes half stumbling into the room, "This shit is so pure. Holy fuck." I had forgotten the plate Anne was holding with coke on it from months ago, and she had tried some of it.

"Wow, where did you get that?" I stammered.

"On this plate in your kitchen," She smiled so innocently.

"I completely forgot about that. It has been in there a very long time."

"Well, that makes sense because it seems a bit stale. It is stuck to the plate in spots. Wanna play a little." Anne starts to pull off her top.

Now, how is a guy supposed to say no to that? There was not much left, so we split it up on the plate and took turns snorting it. Then we turned to our carnal desires. By the time we were finished with each other, we had taken a shower and then headed to the

shop. I was a little late for my appointment, but no harm, no foul. Everyone was

pleased. John grumbled a little about me being late, but it was nothing more than usual.

Anne had called in for the day off, so he was not pissed at her. The tattoo took me an

hour and a half. I charged them for one hour since I was a little late. I told John that

Anne and I would take off early when cleaned up. He grumbled a little, but there was not

much he could do about it. We jump on the bike, and I take Anne by her house for some

clothes. After Anne's house, we go back to my house and crash out by the pool under

the arbor.

I have misting nozzles lining the edges of the arbor, so it keeps things nice and cool on

hot days. You get a bit damp, but you are by the pool anyway. The sun was getting

ready to set. I figured we had slept for about an hour, but it was closer to two hours in

real-time. It was eight-forty-five. We got up and decided to go to Vegas on the bike.

Anne found us a room, so we hopped on the bike and mobbed out to Vegas. We got to

Vegas around midnight. I checked into our room and then bounced out on the town.

We went over to the old Vegas strip from back in the day on Fremont.

We played craps at damn near every casino on the old strip. Anne was a master at craps

and won six hundred dollars. I won fifty dollars. It wasn't what Anne won, but I did not

leave any money behind. By the time we got back to the room, it was five in the morning.

We crashed out until one in the afternoon. We had to pay for an extra day, so we stayed

and used the pool and hot tub. We decided to leave first thing in the morning to make it

back to work by noon. We ordered Chinese and ate it in bed while watching a movie.

We left the hotel at six in the morning and had breakfast. We took our time going home, and it was ten in the morning when we rolled into the driveway of my house. We took a shower and changed the bike out for the truck. We went to an early lunch and still made it to the shop by noon.

"Hey John," Anne greeted John as we walked into the shop.

"Did ya hear about Susan?" John smiled at Anne and me.

"No. What happened?" I was waiting for something terrible.

"She called and said she was retiring because she was getting a million-dollar settlement from her car crash!" John was smiling from ear to ear, "Call her and congratulate her, Chris."

"We are going to go to her house right now!" I slapped John on the shoulder.

"Hold up, Chris, and I will go with you." John started grabbing some stuff and telling the others he would be back.

We all piled into my truck and headed to Susan's house. Sam called me while I was driving, and since I didn't answer, he texted me that he had a hundred thousand dollar check for me at his office. Man, when it rained, it poured. Good shit, man, good shit. We ran up to the door and banged on the door, yelling at Susan. "Susan! We are hungry! Come out and feed us bitch." We all yelled together.

"You sorry fucks. Can't you feed yourselves?" She answered the door in her pajamas, "Come in, so my neighborhood doesn't go to shit assholes."

"Let's go eat!" I try to pull her out the door.

"No, dumbass. I have to get dressed first, at least change clothes." Susan hops up and goes into her room. It only takes her a couple of minutes to change clothes, and she comes out in her sweats and a Sullen tattoo shirt.  "Okay, ready. Where are you taking

me?"

John speaks up, "How about a hamburger at In-n-Out?"

"Nope.  I am too good for that low-life food now," Susan breaks out laughing, "Come on

fuckers I will feed you. Hey, John, can I borrow some cash until I get paid?"

"Sure. Anything you want, miss," John winks at her.

"Anything?"

"Anything that won't get me shot by Alicia."

Anne and Susan climb in the back seat of my truck, and John rides upfront with me.  John

tells me to head towards In-n-Out.

By the time we got back to the shop, it was nine in the evening.  We had lunch, then

drove to Santa Monica and had drinks, then ended up having dinner because we drank so

much that we had to sober up a little.  After dinner, we dropped off Susan and didn't get

to the shop until nine.  We blew the whole day with Susan.  I didn't give a shit one way or

the other because I was happy to spend time with Susan.  She said she would more than

likely be back to work tattooing in a couple of weeks.  She had already been practicing on

practice skin to try and build up her strength and endurance.  She said she was still shaky

and could not tattoo very long.  She would get horrible headaches, and her neck would

feel like it was on fire.  She had been practicing by putting the practice skin in weird

positions to try and mimic a client.  I was pretty stoked about her returning to the shop.  I

had not noticed it a lot until recently, and I guess it was because I had my head up Anne's

pussy lately.  The new was worn off it already, and I was ready to return to business as

usual.  Don't get me wrong, and there is nothing wrong with Anne.  It was just that the newness of me dating someone had begun to wear out, and now we were settling into a comfortable relationship.  It was odd because I had not been in a relationship in years.  It had been five or more years since my last relationship.  The last one ended because I was strung out and had to go to rehab.  My girl at that time was not ready to go into sobriety, so I kicked her to the curb along with my drug habit.  It has been bothering me that Anne might like the drug scene a bit too much.  I had no idea that she even did anything like that before this trip to Vegas.  I am hoping that it was just a fluke and not a habit.  I won't lie about the drug thing scaring me.  I am afraid that I will fall back into the whole drug scene.  I mean, I love getting high on cocaine.

Anne ended up going home and staying there for once.  She said that she had not been at her house in so long that she was afraid that squatters would inhabit it.  Anne usually stayed the night at my house and went home to get dressed for work.  I am sure she had laundry to do.  I was glad to be home alone for once.  I cleaned up and did some laundry.  My gardener had left his bill on my front door a week ago.  The only reason I saw the bill on the front door was that I was looking for the spray nozzle to the garden hose.  I wanted to wash down the back areas around the pool.  I started to call him up and then realized that it was late.  I walked back through the house with the spray nozzle and looked at the clock as I walked through.  It was midnight, and here I am washing the concrete down at midnight.  My neighbors will think that I am back on the dope again.  I place the nozzle next to the water hose and go back into the house.  I wait for my clothes to finish in the washing machine and then put them in the dryer.  I go to bed after I am finished putting the clothes in the dryer and getting them started.

My bedroom seems so lonely, and for once, I realize that I miss Anne being here with me to help silence the loneliness.  Maybe I should ask her to move in with me, dooming the relationship.  Maybes ran through my mind until I fell asleep.

# Five

I woke up at nine-thirty in the morning.  I took a shower.  I retrieved my clothes from the laundry, folded them, and put them up. I went back into the kitchen naked to get some coffee.  As my coffee was brewing, I dressed and went back to my room.

My phone rings, and it is Sam. I don't feel like talking to anyone right now, so I let it go to my voicemail.  I have to go get that check this morning.  I should probably get an offshore account in the Caiman Islands to deposit this money.  That would also give me a place to put the money I found.  I just did not know how to go about doing this. I guess I could ask Sam about it.  I just could not tell him too much about where I got it.  I obviously could not tell him how much money was involved.  The more I thought about it, the more it seemed to be a problem.  I would never have thought that this would be my problem with this cash.  It was not like I could go buy anything significant without causing a lot of attention.  It was bad enough that I fixed my motorcycle up.  John had been asking me all kinds of questions about where I got the money to update my bike.  I told him that I saved and worked on some trade deals with Frank.  John did not believe any of it.  So, here I am with a million, literally a million dollars, and I cannot even spend it without creating a problem.  Maybe I could get John to help me by giving him some of it.  John was good with money, and he most likely knew how to hide money.  I should have asked him a long time ago about what to do with all this cash. I could tell him that I had found a million instead of a million-five.  Why not tell him about all of it?  I hate having this issue. John is right about me not being very good with money.

The more I thought about it, the better the idea seemed to be.  Sam is an attorney, which is as close to the law as I want to get and would not be an excellent choice to talk about the cash.  On the other hand, John is like a brother and should be the person I can trust. Fuck.  I guess there is no hurry.  Meanwhile, I have to go get that check from Sam, and I have to put that cash somewhere other than my bank, which is a cold hard fact.

Sam was not at his office when I went to go the check.  His secretary handed me the envelope and went back to work.  Now I am back to the beginning about what to do with this damn money.  I had to ask John what to do about all of this mess with this cash.  It is not like it is ten thousand or something.  This is big money, and I have no idea what to do with it.  I need help in the worst way.

I texted John and asked him to meet me at one of our favorite restaurants by the shop.  I told him to come alone and not tell anyone he was meeting me, and he would think I was going over the edge again.

I got to the restaurant and waited for John to show up.

 I thought I would go crazy before John got to the restaurant.  I thought about leaving and not telling him.  By the time I dared to walk out, he had walked in. John saw me right away because out of habit, and I am sitting where I always sit at this place.  John walked over with a scowl on his face. John sat down, and the waiter brought John his usual sweet tea.

"So, Chris. What is the problem?"

"Wow, right to the point."

"Well, I have the stuff to do today, Chris.  I hope this is important."

"There are a million reasons it is important," I smiled at him, but he continued to scowl at me.

"Ok. What is it? Let me guess, and you got Anne pregnant. Or some other childish thing. When are you ever going to grow up, Chris?"

"Wow. Am I that big of a fuck up?  Why are you so angry at me?"

"Never-mind. What is this important thing?"

"Well, I came upon a million dollars and two kilos of pure cocaine. There it is out; I have finally told someone."

"What the fuck did you just say?"

"Remember that crash on the corner? The cartel was involved. Cash, cocaine, someone shot someone and stole their stuff?"

"What the fuck, Chris?  Did you shoot someone? The cartel?  What the fuck? You have lost your mind!"

"Hold up. I didn't shoot anyone. Let me explain what happened, and don't interrupt me until I am finished, okay?"

"Ok. You better make this good."

I look at the clock, and it is two hours later. I have been trying to explain the whole thing to John. I told him where I put the money and the coke.  I told him I had not spent much of the cash.  I told John about Susan's house, motorcycle, and Anne, and I asked John for help. John did not speak for a long time.  He sat back and drank his tea, just staring at me.

"Are you mad at me?"

"No, Chris, I am not mad. You just have the worst and best luck of anyone I have ever met. This is some crazy dangerous shit. People have died already from this, and I don't want to be on that list."

"So, let's give it to the cops then? Or give it to a charity or something."

"No. Just shut up and let me think this shit through."

John sat there quietly for a very long time. The waiter kept filling up his glass of tea. John's phone would ring, and he wouldn't even answer it. He just kept sitting there quietly. I was getting worried. He picked up his phone and texted a couple of times. He sat there stone-cold quietly, and it was awkward.

John's phone rang, and he looked at the screen and answered it.  He jumped up and walked outside to talk in private. I ordered a beer and waited for John to return, and I must have waited thirty minutes. My phone rang, and it was John.

"Ok. Chris. Listen and do what I tell you to do," I listen to John's instructions. I pay the bill and go straight to the storage and retrieve a million of the money and one kilo of cocaine. I go to the location that John asked me to go to. The location is an old stock market broker's building in downtown Los Angeles. I have to go through a security gate to get into the parking structure where John meets me at the elevator downstairs in the parking garage. I follow John with the duffel bag full of cash and coke.  We take the elevator up to the penthouse office. I am so nervous, and I am afraid I am getting ready to be murdered. The elevator opens up into a brightly lit office with a view of Los Angeles. John led me to a desk, and I put the bag on the desk.

"Have a seat, Chris; I am a colleague of John's. I am Richard." He leans in to shake my hand. I have a seat by John. Richard unzips the bag and begins to look through the bag. Richard gets up, goes into another room, and comes out with a rolling table with several cash counters.  He rolls it over to the desk and loads cash into the counters. When Richard gets to the coke, he places it to the side and counts the cash. Richard turns to John and me and slides a paper across the desk with some numbers on it.

"What is this, John?" I look at John.

"Well, Chris, the top number is the total amount that was counted. The other figure is a fee for laundering the cash. The last figure is how much clean cash you would have. I am not sure what the last figure is, Richard?"

"Well, John is correct; the last figure is the amount of clean cash you would have if you traded the cocaine for partial service of laundering said money. Any questions?

"Yeah, I have a question. Where does this clean money go to?"

"Good question Chris. The clean money will be deposited into an offshore account in your name. The cash can accrue interest, and if you leave it there in the account, it will double in nine to ten years. Any questions?"

"Chris, this is the fastest and safest way to launder this cash and get rid of the cocaine. Your hands are clean if you should choose to do this, and I strongly recommend you do this," John looks at me.

"Well, John, if you say this is the best way to take care of this, then so be it. When will it be finished?"

John looks at Richard, who answers. "The cash will be in an account by the end of the month, a couple of weeks. We need to fill out some paperwork for the account. John will have to take you over to the bank that I use in the Caymans, so they can be introduced to you."

"What about John? How much should I give you, John?"

"That is included in the laundering fee, Chris. I get a finder's fee per se. Is that okay?"

I shake my head yes towards John. John agrees with Richard, and we start the process. John and I leave Richard's office and go down the elevator to the parking garage. John sends me home, and he goes into the tattoo studio to finish up the day.  It is seven o'clock now. I go home and call Anne as soon as I get to my house. I feel so relaxed now that the big part of this mess is behind me. I still have a couple hundred thousand in storage and a kilo of cocaine. I also have a one hundred-thousand-dollar check to deposit to the new account. I can just use the rest of the cash a little here, a little there. The coke I will find some biker connection and sell it to them.  I got this now that the big part of the cash is deposited somewhere; I am okay.

Anne came to the house around eleven o'clock. We ate at the dinner table and talked about the shop and Susan.  Anne was curious about what John and I were talking about, and I told her it was shop stuff. She believed me and stopped asking about it. I found a movie playing at the theater on the internet, and I cast it on the flat screen. We watched a movie and ate popcorn, and snuggled together. Anne fell asleep about three-quarters through the movie, and I finished the movie and woke her up.  She followed me to bed. All of a sudden, the world seemed to be going in the right direction for me, for once. Anne brought me breakfast in bed. She awoke me with a tray of food and a smile. I asked her to go on a trip with me to Europe to a tattoo convention. She said yes, so I would have to ask John if that was cool. The morning seemed to float on by, and we left for the shop early. My appointments went by quickly. I had two long tattoo appointments that were five hours each and an hour break in-between them for lunch. That means an excellent three-thousand-two-hundred dollars for me. After finishing up around midnight, Anne helped me clean up my booth.

Anne told me John was good with her going with me to the tattoo convention in London. John told her he would arrange all the flight tickets and hotel stay. Everything is going my way. I am one lucky bastard.

# Six

Susan, Anne, and I will be going to London for the tattoo convention.  We will be staying at the same hotel. We will be tattooing together as usual.  Susan and I have been doing this for years, and I enjoy doing the conventions with Susan. This will be nice having Anne there with us to handle all the paperwork and payments. Anne can also help with setup and cleanup to make the tattooing smoother. She can get Susan and me food or run errands for us. Susan and I were excited to work at the convention together this year.

Susan was her usual complex teasing self, and she offended Anne at least once an hour or more.  Anne came to me several times concerning Susan's harsh bitchy behavior.  Each time I had to reassure her that Susan was just teasing. I told her she had a big target on her back because we were officially dating. Susan was very over-protective of me.  Susan wanted to make sure that Anne could pass the test of being around assholes like Susan and me. Anne would smile, look at the floor, and tell me that she thought Susan hated her.  It wasn't until our last day at the convention that Susan asked Anne if she would mind if Susan gave her a tattoo.  It is something that Susan drew up for the convention, and it did not sell. I told Anne that I loved the piece and that it would be an honor to get tattooed by Susan. Anne accepted.  Susan told Anne that she was now officially accepted by her, but she would still be an ass to Anne because that is how she is with everyone. I nodded in agreement with Susan. If Susan accepted you in her circle of friends, you could handle shit-talking and dished it back to Susan with a smile. Anne still had to learn how to dish it back.

We finished the convention on Sunday. We took Anne on a whirlwind tour of the countryside and even made a trip to Paris. John had booked our return flight on Thursday. He gave us four days to play. This was not normal for John to be so happy and giving, and I guess it is because he gained a hundred thousand out of the laundering deal. Richard ended up with two hundred thousand and a kilo of cocaine. I am sure it ended up being more than his usual fee, but who cares because it is all free and clear now. I still had a kilo of cocaine and several hundred thousand dollars that no one knew about.

We left London and headed home. John was waiting at the airport for us when we got home. The ride home was quick, and when Anne and I got to my house, we went to bed and crashed for the rest of the evening and did not get up until the following day.

I woke up, and Anne was still sleeping. I got up and took a shower, and made myself a cup of coffee. While the coffee was doing its thing, I went outside to get the paper. I brought the paper inside and threw it on the coffee table. I went to the kitchen to get my coffee. I went back to the living room and turned on the TV. I drank my coffee and started reading the paper. Anne got up and came into the living room and sat next to me on the couch. I got up and made her some coffee.

"Wow, Chris, John is going to be upset,' Anne yelled from the living room.

"What is it?" I came back into the room with Anne's coffee.

"John's friend got shot," she pointed to the article three pages into the B section.

I took the paper and slowly read the article. Richard, the financial guy that helped me, was shot during a drug deal. A shiver went down my spine. I wonder if he told them where he got the drugs before being killed.

"Excuse me, Anne," I got up to go call John. Before I got to my cell phone in the bedroom, John called me.

"Chris. Did you read the paper?"

"Yeah. What do you think?"

"I don't know, and I do know that it is the same stuff that we gave him."

"Do you think he would try to sell it back to the cartel? He is not that dumb, is he?"

"Fuck dude, he is a friend of mine. My guess is something just went south, and someone tried to rob him."

"Sorry, man. I hope that is all it was because we don't want this coming back to us."

"I hear that, but Richard is pretty careful who he deals with. I am guessing this is just a fluke."

"Keep me posted, John, if you hear anything, and I will do the same. I will see you at the shop."

"Cool. See you there."

I hung up the phone and wondered how much I could trust John's judgment of his buddy Richard. I couldn't help having this heavy feeling of impending doom. I just knew that at any minute, the cartel was going to come busting into my home to cut me up with a chainsaw. My heart was racing, and I seemed to have an issue getting myself prepared for work. I tried to stay calm and not let Anne know how serious this was or how fatal this could be.  I was trying to avoid talking to Anne now because I felt I would give away

how worried I was.

"Hey, Chris. What is your problem? Are you okay? Anne was staring at me with her hands

on her hips.

I let out a nervous giggle, "It is nothing. Everything is cool."

"You are so weird. Why are you laughing at me?"

"It is just that you are standing there with your hands on your hips," I shook my head and

kept getting ready.

"Oh. Okayyyy.  Is John okay?"

"Yeah, he is a bit shook up, but he is okay."

We finished getting ready and went to the shop.  Anne wanted to take the motorcycle,

but Richard's death was freaking me out. We took the truck to the shop.  When we walk

in, the shop is busy, and I get straight to work.  My mind is on my clients, and before I

know it, it is eleven o'clock at night and time to go home.  It is relieving to have the day

go by so fast.  John left to go home at ten thirty, so I didn't even talk to him about

Richard.  John was doing okay, or else he would have come and talked to me.

Anne, Susan, and some other artists wanted to go out to one of the local clubs for some

drinks.  We decided to start over by the pier at Santa Monica.  We had a bit of a drive got

a traffic ticket for five miles an hour over the speed limit, but it was worth the drive.  I

walked in my door at three-thirty A. M. with Anne in tow, drunk off her ass.  We crashed

in the bed and did not wake up until eleven A.M. I had not noticed that the house had

been broken into, and the place was trashed when we came in last night.  I do not think

that the robbers broke in while we were there. However, this morning, the house's condition sent cold shivers down my spine.  Now I know that Richard said something

before he died and that I was suspected and most certainly in danger.

Suddenly, I thought about John, and I just knew that he was dead.  I called, and no one

answered.  I started freaking out.  Anne woke up and saw the house, saw how upset I

was, and started crying.

"What did you and John do?"

"Huh? What? Nothing. What are you talking about, Anne?"

"What. Did. You. And John. DO!? Are you fucking stupid?"

"John and I didn't do anything." I turn and walk towards the kitchen to try and collect

myself and calm down. I start looking around, trying to take notice of anything missing.

"It is nothing more than a simple break-in, calm down," too late, I realize that the one

thing you never do is tell a woman to calm down.

"What the fuck? Did you just say that?" Anne was getting started, "John is my family as

well. God damn it. You are as stupid as they say you are." Anne grabs her purse and goes

out the front door. She comes back in and asks for a ride to her house.

The ride to Anne's house was awkward. On the way to Anne's house, John called and

asked if everything was ok. I told him about my house break-in. John asked if there were

any cartel things around? I told him no. There were some DVDs taken and an old

flatscreen TV. They had gone through some drawers, but there was nothing to take

anyway. John asked how they had broken in. I had no answer. I told him I would have to

get back to him after dropping Anne off at her house. When asked what happened, I told

him I would tell him later.

After the police had left and discovered the unlocked sliding door that goes out to the patio by the pool, I called John and told him the whole story. He laughed at me and called me a dumbass. He also said that I needed to learn how to deal with women.

I decided that I needed to clear my head, so I went for a ride on my bike. I needed that ride more than I could imagine. It felt great going down the highway one by the ocean.

# Seven

The break-in at my house turned out to be kids from the neighborhood. They had broken into several houses. Mostly they stole DVDs and electronics. They came through the sliding glass door. Mine had been the easiest as I had forgotten to lock it the last time I used it. There was nothing evil about the break-in after all. Anne was still mad at me even three days later. Apparently, the "calm down" comment triggered a massive blowout. Every time I saw her, I apologized. On the third day, she acted as if nothing had even happened. I think this is why I have never been able to stay in a relationship for any length of time. I do not understand women, and I do not have patience.

It had been a couple of months since our little blowout and the break-in. The shop was running smoothly. Anne and I were doing great. John had started doing financing for the tattoo shop. The shop was bustling. Mick has been taking Suzy Qs spot permanently since her retirement. Sam had all the paperwork done for Mick's work visa finished. Mick had six years to enjoy us here at the shop.

John wanted us all to have a shop meeting. I'm not too fond of shop meetings. We were taking the whole day off, which meant nothing good was coming out of this meeting. We all asked about the meeting, but John was tight-lipped about it. We will find out tomorrow.

The day drug by so slowly. The tattoos seemed to take forever. I hate meetings, and I yelled out that I hate meetings. The whole shop erupted like a bunch of chimpanzees hooting and hollering. John laughed and said, "Just wait for it, you bunch of heathens." More hooting and howling.

Anne and I went home and snuggled in the bed, watching movies. I don't even know how it happened out of the blue, and I asked her to marry me. Yeah, I was surprised too, and she said yes. Now I have my news for the meeting tomorrow. Fuck, John, and his meetings. We slept great and got to the shop early.

Everyone was early, except John. I am so irritated because I don't like meetings. John finally gets there and acts as nothing has happened. He just goes to his office like we are not having a meeting. Finally, I go get him. And this fucker says, "I thought you hated meetings?" John laughs and then comes out to start the meeting.

John turns on the TVs and tunes them all into the same channel, the computer. John starts a presentation. The presentation is about the Inked Life Tattoo Tour, and we all start bitching about it. Stuff like fuck these guys, and fucking sellouts, shit like that. As the presentation goes on, though, we notice our shop name, which features three of our names.

We all stand up, "What the Fuck?" We all yell together.

"Oh, you fucking sellouts," John laughs. You guys are going on the tour. All three booths are paid, hotels are paid, and the three of you will be tattooing on tour. Anne will go to keep you animals in line. You can take three other artists with you, so, in other words, the whole shop. I will stay here with Suzy Q, who will come out of retirement to help me with the guest artists filling in for you guys. Enjoy the work vacation. You all earned it.

We were all yelling and babbling with each other when we realized that John was gone. I look in his office, no John. I looked in the parking lot, and there he was, smoking a big cigar.

"You, mother fucker." I walked over to him, laughing.

"You like it?" He smiles and winks.

"When did this all happen?" I ask.

"Remember the finder's fee?" He asks, and I nod my head yes. "Well, I thought this would be a nice way to say thank you. So, fucking, thanks." He slaps me on the back.

"Wow. Just, fucking, wow." I shake my head, "I thought I was going to outdo your meeting with my engagement announcement to Anne, but I guess not."

John's eyes widen, "You, fucking, did not?" I nod yes. "You, mother fucker." John punches me in the arm.

We walk back in, and John tells everyone he is not finished with the meeting yet. He was letting us soak it all in, and John has printouts with all the information for them to read. Then he drops my engagement to Anne.

The guest artists will be starting tomorrow. We need to clean up our stations and pack and prepare for the tour that starts next week in Los Angeles at the convention center. We have the week off if we want. John has already arranged our appointments and pay. All plane tickets and reservations were finished and paid in our names.

Everyone starts cleaning up and planning to tattoo at the convention. I go into the office with John, and he shows me all the numbers and plans. The shop made over one million last year. He set money aside for wages, flights, food, etc. He felt we all deserved it.

The supply truck stops by and unloads the supplies that John ordered. We all help out to get the supplies put up quickly. At three PM, we finished, so we left to get pizza and beer. We celebrate our tattoo tour and the engagement of Anne and me.

The week flies by, and the staff is excited about the tattoo tour. Our shop and our names flutter on the banners hanging in the front of the convention center. We will be tattooing like crazy! The convention is great for the shop and the wallet. Super awesome! Suzy Q says she will come by my booth while in LA. The tattoo convention is a three-day tour—Friday, Saturday, and Sunday.

The show is a hit, and we are slammed. We send our overflow to the shop, and they are slammed. Suzy Q only makes it out of the shop for three hours to see me. It reminds us of the early conventions in the UK. Those conventions were vast and busy. I make more money at this convention than any other I have ever attended. We met many of our old tattoo friends from all over the world at the convention. We hung out in the bar at the convention center. This tour looks like it will be a fantastic gig. The weekend is over, and it is time to go back to work.

I called John, and he says the shop hit a record number of tattoos in one day! We close the tattoo shop early and celebrate at the local pizza shop on Monday. It is 3 Am when we leave the place, and time for bed.

# Eight

The tattoo tour was a huge success, and it ended at Daytona Bike Week. We were all tired and ready to get off the tour. It was much more complicated than we thought. We made a ton of money, but we were exhausted. John has been talking about opening another tattoo shop. I am not ready for that at all. However, John can be very persuasive. He plans four more tattoo studios in the Los Angeles and the Inland Empire areas. He says he can do it by staffing the other studios with experienced artists and guest artists. Suzy Q says she will help manage the business. I was too tired to argue, so I told him OK. I say we will discuss it when I get home.

I get home on Tuesday exhausted. John picks us up at the airport and is super excited. He has expanded our LLC to include four more studios with branding and licensing. He talks a mile a minute, and I am too tired to listen. John drops us off at home and says, good night, we are going to bed. I will figure it all out tomorrow. There is always tomorrow, I think as I drift off to sleep.

I got to the shop early today, taking a walk-in tattoo. A guy named Feo wants a Judas De Tadeo and a Jesus Malverde, and to top it all off, he wants a Santisima with a black robe and a brown candle. Those tattoos are something we do all the time. I have all the stencils, so I sized them up and placed them where he wants the tattoos. The tattoos only take me three hours to do. He is super happy, and I get paid a quick thousand dollars. I asked him what his name means, and he said it means ugly. He says that his real name is Santiago Ramirez- Hernandez. He tells me the fucked-up thing about his name is that his Abuelita (grandmother) gave him that name as a kid. Partly because he was fat and ugly and partly because he had an ugly, mean heart. She said he was evil. He looked mean, so I didn't even question it. He seemed to be a real gangster. We come across those people in the tattoo industry all the time.

Feo thanked me and gave me a five-hundred-dollar tip. Very cool. He says he will come back and get another tattoo. Feo ends up becoming a regular tattoo client, and we end up getting along very well. We talk about all kinds of things, and then he drops the bomb. He asks about the accident at the corner, like, did I see it or know anything about it. I told him that I did not see it. I only know what the police said to me that night about it. I ask him how he heard about it, and he tells me that it is his job to know because he is the Hefe. My blood ran cold. I asked him what really happened. He told me that the dead guy in the truck was shot by his men. The dead man and his crew had stolen drugs and money from the stash house. The guys who stole it were all dead, and the police recovered most of the stolen money and drugs. The police had recovered some from the truck and returned it to Feo. That blew my mind. The cops were in with these cartel guys. Feo said he was offering a reward for the person that stole some stuff from the truck. I started getting very worried and nervous.

Feo left the shop, and I thought I would pass out from relief. I thought these guys had bugged the shop, and I know they had been the ones who sent the police. It was the police that came here looking for the cartel. I don't think I will ever sleep again. When I go home, I will take the rest of that cocaine and toss it in the ocean. I hid the cash at the house in a floor safe hidden under the carpet under my bed.

I feel that I am safe because all the evidence is gone. It is freaking me out that the police are working for the cartel. I knew they were dangerous, but this was another level of danger. I told John I did not feel well and had the flu or something. I am going to stay home for a few days. I need to relax before I lose my mind. I have to keep my shit together before I end up giving us away. I don't need to have my head chopped off over a stupid decision on my part. It is too late to go back and make this right.

It was about a month later, and I had not heard from Feo at all. This guy scares the shit out of me. Gary at the corner store, "Hey, you fucking guy you, I heard that boss guy, some guy named Feo, moved to Santa Maria. "

"Never heard of him," I tell Gary. Gary tells me how the guy would come by and press Gary for information and how he forced him to show him the videotapes of that night. "I told this boss guy that there was nothing on the tapes," Gary shakes his head, "I am scared to death of this man. You never met him?"

"Me? Nah, I don't know him, and from the sounds of it, I do not want to know him." I turn and leave the store. I cannot remember being so happy all my life, and it is like I just got pardoned or something.

I get to the shop whistling and grooving and shit. Everyone thinks I am on something, and I just shake my head, nope. I go to my booth and cry. I have never been more scared in all of my life. John comes into my booth to ask me something and gets freaked out by how I look. I explain it, and he almost collapses as well.

"Chris, you think this is over?" John sits on the chair in my booth and leans towards me.

"John, I think so. I mean, I really hope so." I look at John with tears in my eyes. "I think it

is over." I let out a big sigh of relief.

# Nine

Cinco De Mayo in our part of town is a huge thing. Our streets are blocked off for a parade, and the traffic is outrageous. Lots of DUIs from people who become "Mexican" for the weekend. Lots of really cool car shows, bike shows, and art festivals. It is a massive boom for black and gray art in our tattoo shops. The clients are mostly young urban people that do trendy things. Our regulars are year-round. But many of our Cinco De Mayo customers are Cinco de Drinko people. The same people that come in on Friday the 13th for small tattoos. The Friday the 13th specials have become another big thing for us. We do not charge thirteen dollars. Oh no, we charge one hundred and thirty with six dollars and sixty-six cents tips. We play on the 13 and 666 things. Most of the available tattoos are 13 or 666 related. It is a great marketing ploy that slams the shop on those days.

Of course, Cinco De Mayo specials are related to Mexican black and gray art. Lots of Santisima's/ Santa Muerte, Jesus Mal Verde, Saint Judas Tadeo, Zapata, and other things. We also do a lot of Aztec designs on this day as well, and it is one of my favorites because I love this kind of artwork.

Mikail and I were outside smoking cigarettes watching the parade stuff. Susan came outside to slum with us. She is taking over the manager position for John.

"How's it hanging, fuckers," Susan lights a menthol cigarette.

Mikail looks at Susan, "Why do you black people smoke those? They will kill you."

Susan takes a drag and spits on the ground, "So will those unfiltered Camels that you Rooskies smoke, hahaha." She laughs at Mikail.

"Christ on a cracker. Will you two get married already?" I light another cigarette.

A loud bang from the intersection catches our attention. We look over and see a man in a bright yellow shirt get out of a car and approach the pickup he rear-ended. The pickup driver starts to get out of the truck, but as his foot comes out the door, the man in the yellow shirt shoots the truck driver. I mean, he empties the gun in this dude. The yellow shirt calmly walks back to his car, backs up, turns on his blinker, and leaves the scene. People are running everywhere. The truck driver collapsed to his knees with his head on the ground, dead.

We are in shock as we watch the scene. We can hear sirens off in the distance. There is no one around the intersection at this point, and everyone has left. Cars just go around the scene like someone has broken down. It is surreal.

For the next two days, that is all we can talk about. The shooter was found at his house two miles away, smoking a cigarette and drinking a beer in his front yard. The shooter didn't care about the murder or getting caught. The yellow shirt guy said he thought the guy was flirting with his wife, so he killed him. It is the craziest thing I have ever witnessed.

I am not saying we do not see dead bodies, but I have never seen someone executed before in broad daylight. We find dead bodies behind our dumpster around once a year. There are drug addicts everywhere, and you will see how many come out if you are tattooing at night. Like the saying goes, the freaks come out at night.

The pizza place across the street from the shop had a homeless guy that lay dead by the tree on the side of their store for three days before someone noticed he was dead. It can be crazy with the homeless around here. We have a local addict named Joey that passes out on our bench in front of the shop all the time. Sometimes we have to call for EMS because he is too high or drunk. The clients are not bad, though. We have not had the same kind of troubles that my friend Rick has at his shop. Rick is in the Anaheim area, and he has had to fight several people to get them out of the shop because they were spun out on something. That is why we do not allow clients to be drunk or high when we tattoo them. I have only had to toss one client, and that is all. It was not even my client. It seems like the whole tattoo industry has changed. The artists are not as challenging as before, and the clients are not as salty either. Our clients now are professionals like doctors, lawyers, soccer moms, etc. The newer artists come to the industry with hand and face tattoos. When I started in the tattoo industry, the last thing you did was tattoo anything outside of your shirt line. My apprenticeship required making needles, mixing ink, and building my own tattoo machine. Now people just buy everything, and no one knows how to do anything other than a tattoo. Drug addict felons are not prevalent in the tattoo industry anymore. We have them, but not like we used to have. Before, tattooing was kind of left to the outcasts in society. Now many tattoo artists come from art degrees or graphic arts businesses. Ed Hardy showed how successful a trained commercial artist could be in the tattoo world. The industry stood up and noticed. Ed was a real cutting-edge artist that altered his industry.

I am a tiny fish in a massive pond. I know lots of artists worldwide, and they know me. However, I am not in magazines all the time. I still paint and sell art, but I am too lazy to promote myself. In the tattoo world, the one thing that never changed with the industry was that the self-promoted people were the ones that got all the attention. Most of us got into this industry because we love art, and we hate following rules, especially corporate rules. We sleep in, show up late, we are flakes, but we are good at heart. At least that describes me.

I get to the shop late today as usual. I get yelled at as usual. I am the quintessential tattoo artist. I am tattooing a back piece of a Tibetan skull that I drew. It is all color with lots of flames and gold accents. I will start off with a stencil of the skull on the back. The stencil is so large that it takes up six sheets of 11x14 stencil paper. After outlining the skull, I will hand draw the rest of the flames, clouds, and wind bars. This tattoo will take eight hours for the first outline session. After that, my client will come in for four-hour sessions until we are finished. It usually takes between fifteen and thirty hours, depending on the details in the tattoo and how big the person's back is.

Susan comes back to see my progress on the drawing, "how is it coming out?"

"It is coming along," I move and let her see the drawing, "What do you think?"

"Hmmm, it looks great. If you like shit, that sucks," Susan giggles and walks off.

I would expect nothing less from Susan. That means she likes it. She yells back across the shop, "When are you going to tattoo me, asshole?"

"You want me to tattoo your asshole? I will tattoo you when my drawings are less sucky," I laugh at her, "You say when."

"When!" She yells, and the conversation ends. We have been tattooing each other for years. She still has one bare leg that she says is mine if I can learn to draw something she likes. On the other hand, I have only small areas with no tattoos.

I finish up and call my client to come back and look at the drawing before we put the stencil on.

Troy is over in his booth tattooing some girl's butthole. Yup, her purple starfish. And what is she having tattooed on that tender spot, you ask? A rose. She wants a rose on her rose. I guess she is some anal queen and thought it would be funny to have a rose tattooed on the anus. I guess her shit will smell like roses now. She is face down, ass up spreading her cheeks, and Troy is over there with his face in her crack tattooing away while she moans like someone is banging her.

Susan yells at Troy to tell his drama queen to cut out her porn moaning and suck it up and be quiet. Troy laughs and yells at Susan. "You are fucking brutal, Susan!"

Troy was from Amsterdam Susan, and I met him at a tattoo convention. Troy asked if he could come to America and tattoo with us sometime. That was over a decade ago. Troy would tattoo anything because he didn't care it was a penis or a vagina or anything else. You could always count on Troy to do the things that others were uncomfortable doing. This reputation got around the area where we are located, and one of the local pimps used to bring his girls in for Troy to tattoo. He was tattooing "Property of" down one lip of the girl's vagina and tattooing "Estaban" down the other lip. This used to make Susan so angry. Troy said it was money, and he didn't care, but Susan kept at him until he stopped doing it. Troy told the pimp that he could not do those tattoos anymore.

A radio station called and asked Troy to tattoo a guy's balls. Troy didn't care and told the guys to come on down to the shop, and they would do it. They came down to the shop, and Troy tattooed a Lipton Tea label on the bottom of the guy's sack. Troy doesn't care.

# Ten

Anne comes to the shop with me early. My appointment is coming in at nine am, and it is going to be a marathon day of tattooing. When I have big tattoos like this, I only book one tattoo. My client comes in and pays me three thousand cash for the day. I love cash appointments because it keeps the tax man away. Anne had an ice chest with drinks and snacks for my appointment, and we ordered sushi for our lunch. My client is buying sushi for us both because I am very spoiled by my clients.

"Ok, come on back. I hope you are ready for this," I walked towards my booth with my client following me. "Get naked."

"Hey, I even had my Ol' lady shave my back for you," my client Juan straddles my electric tattoo chair that doubles as a table; he leans forward. I raise him up to my level while I am standing, and I will outline half of the tattoo standing up, and then I will finish the bottom half sitting down.

I prepare his back for the stencil of an Aztec calendar. I have him stand up to put the stencil on. We get the stencil on straight and then allow it to dry. I spray some ink-setting fluid on the stencil and allow that to dry as well.

"I am going to draw the rest on you right now," I tell him as he leans into the top half of the chair. He has his earphones in and can't hear me. So, I just started drawing. I think this will be a long tattoo if he listens to music. I finished the drawing and sprayed some stuff to protect the drawing. While it dries, I go up front to see if someone else is there yet. Susan comes in, and I ask her to hang out in my booth with me so I have someone to talk to.

"Oh, are you lonely," she mocks me.

"Actually, yes, I am; wanna hang out." I smile really big for her.

"Ok, as long as Anne doesn't get jealous," Susan pats Anne on the butt.

"Oh, you can have him today. Sharing is caring," Anne winks at Susan.

Susan and I go back to my booth, and she hangs out with me while I tattoo. We joke around, and the time flies by faster. At lunchtime, my client orders sushi for Susan as well. We eat and then go back to tattooing. It is dark when we finish. My client slept most of the time while I tattooed and talked to Susan.

He loves his tattoo, and he tips me fifteen C-notes. I am stoked.

"Hey, Anne, you and Susan want to go get drinks? My treat! Or my clients treat." I wave the cash in my hand.

"Sure. I could use a few drinks," Anne agrees.

"You two kids go get drinks; I am going to go home. I am tired, and my back hurts." Susan rubs her back, and I know she is not joking. She has all but stopped tattooing at this point.

I go to the store to get an energy drink and a pack of smoke. A blue Maserati is sitting in front.

"Hey, who is driving a Maserati?" I yell as I walk in, expecting to see the new girl.

"What's up, mudda facka," Gary pokes his head around the corner. He was rummaging around in the storage closet. "You like my car?"

"That is your car? Damn, Gary, coming up in the world." I turn to look out the window at the car.

"Yeah, I bought it for my dad at the auction. He didn't like it, and he likes his old Jetta."

Gary shrugs his shoulders, "So, now I have to drive it."

"Oh, that is torture," I shake my head. We talk about the shooting at the intersection.

"Hey. Wanna see the shooting on the video?" Gary is all excited.

"No, I saw it all happen in person." I waved him off.

"Ok," Gary is disappointed.

"Fuck it, let's watch it again," I don't want to disappoint Gary. So, we watched the video about six different times. Then I went back to the shop.

By the time I get back, it is closing time. Susan decides to go home, and Anne and I do the same thing.

"Hey, Susan, did you know Gary bought a Maserati?"

"Where have you been, Chris? He bought that last month." Susan laughs at me and walks out the door to go home.

# Eleven

When you have kids, you do many crazy things to support them. When you have kids and are a tattooer, you get foolish and creative when you support them. So, when John's kids had a crab feed at their school to raise money for the booster club, John asked all the shops to come to the event and donate some money to the club. John paid for all the tickets for everyone to go. We ended up buying four whole tables at the event. John Jr. had actually baked a cake for a friendly competition with the other kids in his group. One of the kids had their cake featured in home and gardens magazine, and the kid got one thousand for his cake! The kid was from a very influential family. We could not let that go unanswered. So, our dirtbag crew of tattooers pooled all our money and ended up paying three-thousand dollars for John jr.'s cake. The look on the faces of that kid and his family when Johnny's cake beat him out was priceless.

We cut the cake up and tried it. A three-thousand-dollar cake, and it tasted like shit. Hahaha, Johnny can't cook for shit. We told his daddy John that he owed us money. The funny thing is John paid us all back! Hahaha, what a maroon.

Johnny jr. graduated that month, and they took a trip to Cancun, Mexico. The shops were doing great. John had people trained and working as managers at each studio. John just did the business of running the corporation side of things. John had everything arranged for his trip.

As John said, the family would be gone in two weeks, and then it would be back to the grind.

Anne and I took them to the airport, and we would be there to pick them up when they were all finished. John promised to check in every other day, and I kept telling him that we were okay, and we got this no matter what.

"Relax, John, we got this. Holy shit, dude, it is not that hard," I pat John on the shoulder.

"I know, Chris, but I just get worried because things get out of whack so easy. You will tell me if you need anything?"

"Yes, now get the hell out of here." John and the family took their luggage and entered the airport. As soon as they went inside, Anne and I took off.

"Don't you think we should go inside?" Anne asked me concernedly.

"Hell no, we can't park here anyway. It is a drop zone, not a parking zone." I pointed to a sign that said no parking.

"I want to go on another trip. Like we did to Europe for the convention. Please?" Anne gave me the puppy dog eyes.

"Yeah, sure. Whatever you want," I said to get Anne to be quiet. Although, I would like to do that convention again.

The drive home was easy. We went to a nice restaurant on the beach on the way home. I promised that we would try to take a trip when John returned home, and Anne was okay with that.

The following week went by really well, and John called every day. Susan got mad and told him not to call her again until he got home, "You are on vacation, asshole, act like it." So, John stopped calling.

The shop is so busy that none of us have had time to watch TV, let alone the news.  One of our clients walked in and asked if we had the news on our flatscreens in the shop, and Susan turned it on and found the channel the guy was looking to watch.

John is staying at the resort where the cartel shot twenty people.

"I will call," Susan said. I have his number and the hotel number, and John did not answer his phone. We all waited in surreal horror as the resort answered, and Susan asked about the shooting.

"We cannot give out that information at this time," the man on the phone was very polite. "We will be notifying relatives in the next couple of days, and we are sorry."

We left the news on, and the shop was silent. People finished the tattoos they were working on and canceled their other appointments. The news station offered no names, only a body count. A local cartel had been extorting the resort for protection money. The cartel came onto the resort property when the resort refused to pay. Cartel members killed the manager, the bartenders, and approximately twenty guests on the private beaches of the property. There was very little information. The government had shut down cell service for some reason. My stomach was knotted up, and I felt like I would be sick. Anne and Susan came and sat down next to me. Pretty soon, the whole shop was huddled in a circle watching the horror play out.

We sat watching the news all day, trying to see if we could notice anything as the cameras panned the beaches showing a body here and there on the beaches. Maybe they were up in their room or out on a scuba diving trip or something.

At eight pm, the news had a breaking report that a bus had been attacked. The bus was taking tourists to some of the ruins in the area. Again, the report lacked any other information. People began to trickle home early, so we locked up the shop and went home. Susan came to my house with Anne and me. We sat on my couch and watched the news until we fell asleep on the couch together.

The phone woke us up at seven forty-five am; Anne answered the phone.

"Hello, yes, this is Anne Yepez. Si, mi hermana es Alicia Sanchez. Si. Oh, my God. Ok, si," Anne was sobbing at this point. She hung up the phone, "John is dead. Oh, my God, Chris," Anne shook as she cried.

"What about Alicia and the kids," Susan asked.

"Alicia is in the hospital in critical condition. John Jr. was shot in the foot, but it is ok. And Tammie is ok," Anne buried her face in a pillow.

The wave of horror washed over me. It was not real, I kept telling myself. People like John just didn't die like this. We sat hugging each other, waiting for more information. The phone rang again, and I answered, and I wanted some information to damn it. It turns out John was at the bar getting drinks and was shot when the bartender was shot. Alicia was on the beach with the kids waiting for a drink. When the shooting started, she tried to cover the kids with her own body. She was hit in the back of her shoulder and butt. John Jr.'s foot was hit as well. Tammie was protected by her mom.

I can't understand how this could happen. So much needless death. How could my culture be so evil? This was going to be hard to process. The next few months proved to be more complicated than we thought possible. John Jr. and Tammie were sent home to be their Nana Yepez. Alicia would come home a month later after being released from the hospital. All of them got home before John's remains made it home. They sent his ashes. They fucked around lagging on everything and ended up cremating John. Their answer was that he could not have an open casket anyway, and they had to investigate the crime. It was a lot of bullshit added on top of the horrific death of my cousin/brother.

I have been useless these past months while Susan has been the company's savior. She stepped up into John's job and ran this company like a general. The whole business would have collapsed, and I would not have given a shit. I am still sober, and the only reason is Anne. I found out this morning that I was going to be a dad. Anne is pregnant. My brother is not here to share this with me, and it is killing me.

Anne and Susan are the glue that is keeping all of us together. I have never witnessed such strong people other than John. Alicia and the kids are back at home, coping with the loss of John. We go by to see them every other day. I keep thinking that we will never recover from this. Alicia is still on a walker, and John jr. is still on crutches. Tammie seems oblivious to everything that is going on. Susan says it is the only way that Tammie can cope.

Everyone is happy about the new baby. We will find out if it is a boy or girl soon; it has already been decided that we are naming the baby after John, and we will be using his middle name, Patrick. Sadly, I have to remember him this way.

I have been drinking too much, and Susan says they will send me to rehab soon. Susan means business, and she keeps me together. I have been taking rides along the beach lately to try and ease my mind. My art sucks lately, and it is like my imagination died with John. Mikail at the shop told me to suck it up and stop being a little bitch. He said John would be fucking pissed at the way I was quitting life.

# Twelve

It has been six months since John passed. My art is coming back to me, taking on a darker tone. The strange thing is that everyone likes it more. I am the new Aztec version of Paul Booth, I wish. I am finally back into the swing of things, and Susan has booked me solid for the next eight months. I throw myself into my art to save myself. Tattooing is keeping me alive at this point. I know it is stupid to say, but I am depressed. John Jr. is going to go to UCLA in the spring. Tammie is in her senior year, and she seems to be doing great. Alicia and the kids have been seeing a counselor; she says it is to help them deal with life, she says I should go with them, and I tell her that I will think about it. We got the news! We are having a girl, and her name will be Patricia Analice Yepez Hernandez. We fancy now. Who would have thought that I would be a father? Anne says that I will make a great father.

A client, Lupe, called me today about doing a backpiece for him. Lupe wants one of my Aztec-style skulls with an Aztec temple in the background. Lupe is six foot five and is super wide across the shoulders, and it is going to be the most enormous tattoo I have ever done. He says he wants to tattoo his chest and stomach as well. Dollar signs float in my mind as I think of an elaborate tattoo for the back and the front. Gotta get 'em while you can, upsell the shit out of your art.

Frank is here for his last session on his backpiece. He asked me to ride the bike to work today. A bike magazine wants to interview Frank and me, and they will take pictures of the bike and Frank's tattoos. It is great exposure for him and me and our work. I am excited about the photoshoot. Things are going well for me, and I am starting to come out of my funk.

Rick "R2" and Mikail come riding into the shop's parking lot with two black and whites following with their lights on. They are both freaking out because R2 has a warrant and no license, and Mikail has let his visa expire. Both of their bikes are impounded, and they get citations for speeding. R2 gets another driving on a suspended, but they do not arrest him.

"Holy hell, R2. What did you guys do?" I patted him on the shoulder. Mikail is as white as a sheet.

"We were splitting lanes down the 101 at eight per." R2 was laughing.

"I didn't think they would catch us," Mikail was laughing, "but this asshole can't ride for shit." He points to R2.

"Fuck you, Miki, ya commie bastard," R2 laughs at Mikail. "Mikail thought this was like Russia, and he was going to prison for life."

"You are a liar, R2," Mikail points his finger and R2.

Soon, everyone in the shop is watching them load up the bikes to take to impound.

"How many bikes have you sent to impound, R2?" Susan asks him.

"I don't know. At least four this year." He shrugs his shoulders. "My fines are around ten thousand now, and I will never get my license back."

Mikail teases R2, "That Is why you are always getting caught. You buy shitty bikes."

"Yeah, well, your bike is gone this time." R2 laughs.

"You are right, R2, you are right," Mikail shakes his head sadly, "I still owe on my bike. How do you get them back?"

R2 points to me, "Ask Chris; he knows how."

I nod my head, "I will help you get it out of impound. We should be able to get it out after three days."

The cops and tow trucks leave us standing there in front of the shop. We all end up around my bike, smoking and joking. I go inside with Frank, and we finish his backpiece. The guy from the magazine takes some great photos of the tattoo, and he is going to send them to several tattoo magazines as well. After all the photos are finished, we sit in the breakroom, and he does the interview.

The interview brings up a lot of my childhood trauma, the death of my parents, my homeless days, my druggie days, and my years of becoming the artist I am. He leaves off the death of John; Frank gave him a heads up that the topic was a "no-fly" zone.

Frank talked about growing up in Tijuana and East LA. He talked about getting into the custom bike scene with his drug addict uncle. Then they talked about Frank's prison sentence that helped him learn how to do paint and bodywork; those classes started him in the business he is in now.

"Ask Chris, I was a real dirtbag. Riding with bike clubs and doing crimes," Frank kept talking, "Chris and I partied a few times, and we ran around in the same circles."

The interviewer, Eric, asked Chris, "Was that before your parents died, Chris?"

"Yeah, it was right after they died. I had started hopping trains and riding motorcycles when I could steal one. I had no one at home, so I would crash at Frank's once in a while."

"I thought you were given your parent's house?" Eric pressed.

"They did. I was wild as hell; John took care of everything for me and was trying desperately to calm me down. Susan, our manager, worked with John to get me to pull my head out of my ass. They got me into rehab." I shook my head, remembering how much I owed them for saving me, "I would not be here if it were not for those people."

"What saved you, Frank?" Eric prodded Frank.

"Prison. Prison saved my life. It is a hard reality, but that is what made me who I am."

Frank leaned back in his chair, "We got lucky, didn't we, Chris?"

"Damn skippy Frank." I jumped up. Anxious for some reason and went to the bathroom. I came back out, and Frank and Eric were out front smoking.

Anne gave me a big hug with tears in her eyes, "You are so humble; it is a wonderful thing. I love you."

"Um, thanks. I guess," I don't think that I did anything special other than survive all these years.

Susan chimed in, "Stop making me sound like captain save a hoe." We all laughed at that.

I walked out front and lit a cigarette. "You like that shit?" I pointed to the bike. "Frank hit that shit out of the park. My bike is sick. If you want one like it? Call Frank and have a grip of cash."

It was midnight and time to close the shop. Everyone said their goodbyes. I put my bike

in the shop storage, it is our garage for the shop. Anne drove the truck to the shop today,

so we rode home together.

Anne could not stop talking about how impressed she was with my humbleness.

"Have you met me? I am not humble. How am I humble?" I was frustrated, I guess, and I

said it too loudly.

"Damn, Chris, you don't have to be mad about it. I was just saying what you don't see."

"Well, I did not mean to sound mean or rude; I am just confused about how humble I

am."

"Not one time did you talk about all the hard work that you have done, all the grinding to

get better; instead, you give the credit to everyone else for saving you. Sometimes you

make it sound like you have no talent or motivation."

"I get what you are saying, Anne, but without them, I wouldn't even be here to do

anything with talent."

"Ok, fair enough, but I still get to be in love with you, Chris." She reached over and held

my hand as we drove home.

I guess I do not give myself much credit, and I give credit to many other people. It helps

remind me that I came from the bottom and keeps me grateful for my success.

# Thirteen

Anne and I are parents! Anne gave birth to Patricia Rene Yepez Hernandez, 7 pounds 4 ounces and 19 inches long. I know we changed her name again, hahaha. She has a full head of black hair. This is amazing. Susan and everyone else came by to drop off cards and flowers. Everybody is taking pictures of our new tattoo princess. The hospital is sending them home today. It is going to be weird having a baby at the house. We have fixed up the place, and now it looks like a family house instead of a bachelor's pad. Patricia's room is fixed up with everything imaginable.

I can't wait to take them home. Susan is helping me with the preparations for our homecoming. She is staying at the house while I bring Anne and Patricia home, and Susan is even cooking something for us to eat when Anne gets home.

I pack up the truck and put it in the car seat and the new diaper bag full of everything imaginable. I am slow to get to the hospital because I have started to drive slower in preparation for driving with a baby in the car.

Anne and Patricia are in the room waiting for me. The nurse has all the paperwork ready to sign to release them. They give us a copy of the birth certificate. The nurse pushes Anne and Patricia in a wheelchair to the waiting truck outside.

The nurse sees the truck and wrinkles up her nose, "I hope you are going to get something more reasonable, Chris." The nurse points at the truck.

Anne and I both laugh because we had discussed this when Patricia was born. "Yes, we do need something more reasonable," I tell the nurse.

I am guessing I will be adding another car to the list. Maybe we could buy a nice BMW or Mercedes, and I am sure Anne would like that.

We loaded Anne and Patricia in the truck, and the nurse helped me figure out the car seat issue. She makes me put the car seat in the middle of the back seat. Once everyone has buckled in, the nurse waves goodbye to us.

I have never been more afraid to drive in my life. Anne is laughing at me, "Oh, my God, Chris. You drive like a grandma."

"I can't help it. I am nervous, and I have never had a baby in a car before," my knuckles are white from gripping the steering wheel so tight. I concentrate on driving so much I don't talk much.

Anne laughs at me, and the drive is slow. I finally got to the neighborhood and began to relax. I pull into the driveway, and Susan comes running out of the house. She opens the truck's back door and gets Patricia out of her car seat. I opened the door for Anne and helped her out of the truck and into the house. I go back outside and bring in all the bags. The girls are in the house talking excitedly and ignoring me.

"Chris, bring Anne a soda and me a cup of coffee, please," Susan asks me.

"Oh, while you are in the kitchen, can you bring me some chips? Thank you," Anne asks.

"So, this is life now?" I stand looking over the sink at them, sitting on the couch holding Patricia.

"Yes!" Both Susan and Anne answer. "This is a girl's house now. Get used to it," Susan says.

I get them their drinks and snacks. Susan informs me that lunch is on the stove and that I should make them a plate and bring it into them. I go back to the kitchen, fix a plate, and serve them on the couch. Then I have to go fix the house's temperature to make them comfortable for Patricia, of course. I fix myself a plate and start looking for a car while sitting in the recliner. Patricia whimpers a little bit, and Susan checks to see if she needs to be changed. Susan calls me over to change the diaper and prepare a bottle. She walks me through the whole thing. Anne watches nervously. I do okay, and they tell me I will get better with practice.

"Hey, Anne, do you mind if I go look at a car for us?"

"Sure, Chris, go ahead. I want something sensible like an Avalon or something like that."

Susan chimes in, "Anne does not want a Mercedes or BMW, so get those out of your mind."

Damn it. There goes that idea, and I start looking at Toyotas. "How about a Sequoia?"

"That would be ok, I guess." Anne agreed.

"Avalon gets better gas mileage; a Sequoia gets fifteen miles per gallon." Susan reminds me because I always complain about the truck gas mileage.

So, I narrowed my search down to an Avalon, and I found a white one with five thousand miles. It is a rollback. It is not even broken in yet, but it is cheaper than a new one. I call to check if it is still there. I ask the girls if they want to go, and they both give me a weird look like I am insane.

"Go, by yourself," Susan tells me, "Go do man shit. We will do women's shit. Now go get the girls a car. Men, I swear." Susan and Anne started laughing. "Bye, boy, go on and buy a car."

"I am going already, damn." I laugh at the two of them and go out the door.

The dealer convinced me to trade in my truck. He knows who I am and has a tattoo from

me. I end up leaving my truck there, and I take the car home. It is white with a tan

leather interior. We get the baby seat base buckled into the backseat.

The whole deal from start to finish only takes three hours. The truck is theirs, and the car

is mine. They filled it up with gas and washed it while I was doing the paperwork.

I feel pretty good about the car as I pull into the driveway. I walk into the house all

excited about getting the car, and I want them to see it. That will have to wait because

they are all asleep. So, I sit down to take a nap as well.

# Fourteen

I am sleep-deprived. I miss my truck, and it seems like I cannot think straight.

Everything revolves around my daughter lately, and Susan says that is how life goes.

Anne understood and told me to ride on my bike to get my thoughts in order. I think that

is pretty cool of her. I ride my bike to and from the shop daily, making me feel a lot

better. It really clears my mind.

I think about what I will do when the weather gets shitty and cold. Maybe, I will get

another truck; I miss my truck.

Susan keeps me super busy, and she says it keeps me distracted from all the chaos of

being a parent. Either way, I do not have time to think about anything other than

tattooing. I have to keep on my grind because I have a kid to raise now.

Everything is going well. Life seems to be everything you could want. The business is

booming, I am super busy and making more than ever, and life is great. It scares the hell

out of me.

Susan has arranged for us to do some conventions. I think it sounds great. We will go to

the Queen Mary and have a convention there first, and she has some others planned out

as well.

I like the Queen Mary one because Troy and I can ride over to it. Like we used to do, I

cannot wait for things to get back to the old normal.

I went to the store and saw Gary. He drops a bomb on me by telling me that he saw Feo in town. The cartel boss that we thought was gone for good. It freaks me out so bad that I cancel my last appointment. It is a small appointment, and Susan is angry. She has no idea why I would want to cancel. We even argued about it, and I took off anyway.

I am crabby by the time I get home. Anne is asking me one hundred questions. She and I get into an argument, and things go sideways. I told her I just had a terrible headache and wanted to lay down for a bit.

For the following week, I can't sleep, I can't eat. I am freaking out over this Feo guy coming back into the area, and I can't stop thinking about it.

Troy takes me on a ride to help me clear my head. He asks me what is going on, but I can't tell him. I wished John were here to talk about it because John would know what to do.

Troy and I rode up to Tanks beach, and then we came back into town. It was a nice ride, but I could not shake the worry about Feo. I had dumped the cocaine in the sewer a while back. The money I used for the new car and the rest I deposited into the offshore account. The storage I closed out.

I had Sam help me write a will and get everything sorted out if anything happened to me. Anne does not know about the offshore account. After Sam and I finish up everything, I begin to feel better. I figure if something happens, at least Anne and Patricia will be taken care of.

I tell Anne we need to get life insurance to ensure that we are doing the responsible thing as parents, and she agrees, and we both take out policies. As time passes and I do not hear anything else about Feo, I begin to feel better.

The tattoo shop is getting busier, if that is possible. Everyone is booked solid for a minimum of three months. We do not have any room to take on new artists. Our other tattoo studios are booked out a month in advance as well. The amount of money we are making is obscene. We decided that Susan should get a raise. Anne has been home with Patricia. So, Susan hires someone for the front desk, and she hires a shop helper for the artists.

As things get busier, we hire a shop manager to replace Susan to focus on the corporation. Susan wants me to hire an artist to take my place and go on tour as much as I want. I refuse to do this because I want to tattoo. I cannot think of doing anything else.

Our shop front faces west, and in the morning, we keep our blinds closed to keep the sunlight from heating up the shop. So, it is no surprise when a client comes in and informs us that we have two weirdos out in front. One is in a pink tutu, and the other is dressed like Sailor moon. I go out front with Troy to check it out.

Joey and some other crackhead that just got out of jail are out front. Joey is in a Halloween costume of Sailor Moon with a plastic mask, and the other guy is in a pink tutu with white panties, a pink bra, and orange flip flops from the jail. They are out of it on drugs. Tutu dude is dancing around singing, and Joey is half coherent, laying on the bench in front of the window.

"Joey! Get the hell out of here," Troy kicks him in the leg. The Tutu dude continues singing. "Get the fuck outta here."

Susan comes out of the shop, "I got this, Chris." She carries a bucket of water out the front door and dumps it on Joey, "Clear out, Joey, you know better."

"Damn it, Sue, I am just tired," Joey complains. Tutu dude chimes in, "Yeah, we are just tired.

"Was I talking to you, Fairy Godmother? Get the fuck out of here, I already called PD, and they are on the way." Susan walks back into the shop.

"I would listen to her because she means business. Susan is not going to put up with your shit Joey."

"Aw, come on, Chris, don't take her side," Joey slurs his words. He tries to sit up but is obviously too high to manage.

Police roll into the parking lot. Troy and I went into the shop. Susan meets the officer named Aaron outside and discusses what is happening. Susan comes back into the shop.

"Shit. The officers called EMS because they think Joey is overdosing." Susan is pissed. No one wants this kind of attention on a busy day. Tutu dude is now dancing around the cop car as they attend to Joey, passed out on the bench. EMS arrives and administers Narcan. Joey wakes right up.

"Leave me alone! I don't want to go to the hospital," Joey is yelling at everyone, trying to help him. Tutu dude is singing, "stop, in the name of love, leave Joey here my love, think it o, over" as he dances around the cop car and the EMS vehicles. The scene has become a huge circus.

"I swear to God, this shit is out of pocket," Susan goes into her office and slams the door. Troy is videotaping the scene. Someone pulled up the blinds, and now everyone is watching the local entertainment for the day. Susan comes over the intercom, "Tell me when they are gone."

She is irritated because she has been dealing with Joey for the last three weeks daily. The police don't really do anything about it, but she calls them almost every day to handle Joey and the Tutu dude.

EMS leaves Joey alone, and they get in their vehicles and leave. The police convince Joey and Tutu dude to leave the property. Aaron comes in to talk to Susan about the situation. I led him to the office. Susan brings him into the office and slams the door. You can hear her shouting at Aaron.

Aaron comes out of the office, "Damn, she is angry. Let me know if Joey comes back today. I will trespass him, and he will go downtown for around two hours, and then he will be back out. Sorry, the DA won't prosecute these assholes." Aaron gets in his squad car and leaves with his partner.

We all get back to work tattooing. Susan comes out of her office and calms down a little bit. The shop has 90s rap going, and everyone is grooving. Tattoo machines are buzzing, and people are laughing. The day is going great. Even Susan is calm enough to start joking around with everyone.

The front door opens, "Hey can I have a bottle of water? Joey doesn't feel good. Water will wake him up." The Tutu dude is pacing around all panicked.

"I'll go check," Rick jumps up and goes around back by the dumpster, and Troy follows him. I get curious and go outside as well. Meanwhile, Tutu dude paces around wanting water.

By the time I get to the alley in the back of the building, Rick and Troy are on their way back, shaking their heads, "He finally did it." Troy says as he walks by.

"What happened, "I ask.

Rick answers and points to the dumpster, "Go see for yourself. Joey is dead behind the dumpster, still has the needle in his arm."

"God damn it, Joey," I yell at the dead body of Joey slumped against the side of the dumpster. He is already bluish in color.

Tutu dude runs around in the parking lot screaming that Joey is dead. Rick and Troy delivered the news to Susan, and the Tutu dude heard what they said. "At least the traffic of cops and EMS will be in the alley this time," Susan tells us.

Susan was as wrong as you can get. The police, EMS, Coroner, and the local news station fill up the parking lot. They block the entrances with police tape, and no one is allowed into the parking lot. We all finish up the clients we are working on, and then we have to cancel the rest of our appointments for the evening. Susan is livid.

"Chris, call Sam. See what we can do about them letting Joey go, and then he ends up dead. There has to be something he can do." Susan is raving mad.

"Susan, we all know that nothing will happen. There is nothing he can do about it. It is California policy; it is not the fault of the police." I try to calm Susan down, but I am not getting through to her at this point.

The police wanted Rick, Troy, Susan, and I to stay because we were the ones that interacted with Joey and Tutu dude. This made me angry because they let Tutu dude walk away down the road. The police told him to leave. The police want us, innocent people, to stay, but they allow the guilty party, Tutu dude, to walk away. I can see why Susan is so angry with the police. They make no sense about how they do their job. Susan is outside yelling at the police about their incompetence, and I am letting her go at it. The police deserve it. The inaction of the police and EMS is what caused this to happen. The decision by the police to act like we are at fault is infuriating.

We can hear Aaron trying to calm Susan down, "We are not blaming you, Susan. We just want a full report about what you guys know."

"What? Didn't you take the report from when you were here earlier? Did you include in your fucking report that you let Joey go without taking his drugs from him and his friend? And now Joey is dead. You did that, Aaron; you killed Joey. Fuck you, Aaron," Susan spit at the ground. She was ready to throw hands with Aaron.

"Look, Susan, enough of this. Susan, calm down! I will arrest you for disturbing the peace," Aaron holds his hand towards Susan.

I try to get out of the shop fast enough to stop what is about to happen. Aaron and Susan were in a scuffle when I got out the door, and several other officers are now involved. As I approach, I am thrown down to the ground as well. Susan is being dragged into the back of a squad car. I am handcuffed and sit down on the bench in front of the shop. Rick and Troy watch in amazement at what is going down.

"Call Sam," I yell at Troy. Troy nods his head yes. "Lock up the shop, and I will call you later. Oh, and Call Anne and tell her what is going on." Troy again nods his head.

Troy is calling Sam and Anne. The police tell Susan to stop kicking the window because she is racking up more charges. The parking lot is lined with people from the neighborhood to watch the circus. I try to remain calm. Being calm is my only way of going home at this point. I am pretty sure that I am on my way to the county jail.

The car with Susan leaves the parking lot. An older officer comes over to me and uncuffs me. "Go inside! Keep your mouth shut, and you can go home," he Instructs me as he takes off the cuffs. "Not a word, now. You see, your friend is being taken downtown.

Unless you want that ride as well, shut up." He opens the front door of the shop and lets

me inside.

Rick, Troy, and I sit in the shop until all the vehicles leave. Sam informs us that Susan will

spend the night at the county for a disorderly charge. Sam tells us on the speakerphone

that he will take care of this but tells us to shut the fuck up. We all go home.

# Fifteen

Sam did us all a favor by contacting the news station and convincing them not to run the news report. He bought a copy of the report from the station and explained that this would be evidence for a civil suit for the police department. Sam knows someone at the station. The station uses the segment against the DA and police department for failed policies that punish innocent citizens and businesses instead of drug addicts and criminals.

This segment puts a massive target on our backs. The police are not our friends now for sure. Not that they ever were our friends. If we call about the homeless, the police department either does not show up or arrives eight hours later. The police post up in our neighborhood and pull over clients and artists coming to and from the shop. It gets so bad that Sam files paperwork for an injunction that a local judge upholds.

The police are not finished with us, though. Another homeless person dies behind the business's dumpster next door, and the police shut the whole strip mall down for three days. They say it is for an investigation. We all know they are just messing with us to prove a point. Susan has become a substantial anti-cop fan. She cannot stand the local PD. She tells everyone how she feels. The incident has turned her against the local law enforcement. Sam tries to talk to her about it, but it does not change her mind.

She refuses to call the police for anything. Susan says she is better off paying the homeless to leave us alone. Susan's attitude has a strange consequence. Susan asks the homeless man hanging out beside the shop to wash our windows. The guy agrees, and Susan buys him all the necessary supplies to do the windows twice a week. Susan talks to the property manager and convinces him to hire the guy to do all the business windows twice a week.

Walter, who looks like Magic Johnson, buys a wagon to haul the supplies around with him. Susan lets him store the stuff in our shop storage. He begins to do the windows of the shopping center across the street, and then Gary hires him to do the store. Walter bought a truck; he is living in an apartment. Walter comes in to see Susan with a big bouquet of roses and a thank you card.

"Here you go, Miss Susan." Walter hands the roses to Susan, "Because of you, I have my life back. I now have over two hundred clients that I do windows for. You are the one that started that for me. God Bless you."

Susan stood there speechless with watery eyes, "You are most welcomed, Walter, but you didn't have to get me anything."

"I owe you everything. I thought I was done. No one wanted an old black felon, but you did." Walter was tearing up. "Thank you. You have restored my faith in humans."

Susan gave Walter a big hug. Walter walked out of the shop and went to work washing the windows on the strip mall we were in.

Walter changed Susan. Susan became happier and less angry. Susan and Walter would have lunch together at the sandwich shop across the street every week. Susan helped Walter invest some of his money and helped him set up a business and hire some workers. Today Walter has a window washing service with ten employees. All of this is because of the incident with Joey. We have never seen Tutu dude again. Susan talks about it from time to time. She shakes her head about how the death of Joey ended up changing so many things.

On the following Saturday, we came to the shop, and it was eighty degrees in the shop at eight am. Susan tried to turn on the AC. Nothing happened. She called the property manager to fix the AC because the temperature was too high to tattoo.

I rode up with Troy on our motorcycles to find several AC trucks and police cars. My first thought was, oh shit, not again. But when I walked into the shop, Susan was laughing with a tall, gray-haired officer.

"Hey, Chris, this is officer Torres." Susan points to the officer.

"Hey, you here to arrest Susan?" I teased the officer.

"God damn it, Chris, that is over and done," Susan laughs.

"Um, no. I am here because of the AC thefts." He points to the roof, "Last night, the AC units on this strip mall were stolen."

"WHAT!? All of them?"

"Yes, sir, all of them. I am just making a report for your insurance company." Officer Torres is very professional.

"Isn't he great," Susan gushed. She was into this cop, and it was no secret.

Officer Torres was six foot four at least and very muscular. He looked to be in his early forties. Perfect age for Susan. I stood back and watched the fireworks between the two. Never in a million years would I have thought that Susan would be interested in a cop. He was Hispanic, dark complexion, blue eyes, and a babyface; he looked like John.

"Hey, Chris, can you call everyone and let them know that they should cancel today because of the AC issue. Or they can tattoo if they want, but there is no AC."

"Sure, Susan, you two just finish what you are doing, and I will take care of it."

Troy and Rick brought personal air conditioners that they could plug into the wall in their booths and did not cancel anyone. That was a great idea, so I called the local hardware store and bought one for each booth. Everyone ended up tattooing, and we did not have to cancel appointments after all. Susan was a bit peeved because I think she wanted to flirt with Officer Torres more.

The AC guys fixed our unit first since we needed it more. It was all finished by the end of the day. AC will be working tomorrow for sure. The property manager had the security company install pressure sensors on the roof to set off alarms if anyone got on the roof again. It cost eighty-seven thousand dollars to replace the AC units that were stolen. The property owner hired a security company to check the property from this point on.

Susan was back to her grind at the shop, training for her replacement. Mary was the new manager's name. It took Susan more time to train Mary than she thought she needed to train her. We even took her to a tattoo convention with us to help her understand the workings of our business. Ordering supplies, dealing with artists, using our appointment system, payroll, billing, marketing, hiring, etc. Susan did not expect Mary to be another Susan. Still, she did want her to be as competent as the other managers. Susan connected Mary's salary to bonuses on how well the shop did financially. The bonuses always reeled in the managers and motivated them to be hardworking and successful.

Officer Torres appeared at the convention and got a tattoo from us. After his tattoo was finished, he and Susan disappeared for several hours. Susan and Jesus Torres have been dating, and we found out about it at the convention. He fits in with us and is a cool guy. Not what I expected for a cop. Just goes to show you never really know anyone. Jesus and Susan came back and hung out with us for a while.

I have this couple that comes to us for a tattoo. This chick and this dude she just met. They want each other's names tattooed on them. Only, he doesn't, so he tells her to go first. She decides to tattoo his name right over her pussy because she does not want her parents to see the tattoo. The dude is freaked out about it. He holds her hand as we do the tattoo. The vibration from the machine is getting her all wet.

Suddenly, she squirts. The smell is so bad my eyes water; I fake sneeze, get up and go to our supply container to grab a mask and spray air freshener in it. I tell her I have allergies and don't want to sneeze on her. I know the dude holding her hand catches a whiff as well.  He says he is going to go outside to smoke. He never comes back in. We finish the tattoo, and she goes out to find him because he is her ride. She comes back upset that he left her here. She had to wait for her friend to come and pick her up at the Queen Mary. Now that is embarrassing.

Jesus is getting to see the crazy part of our industry. He and Susan are all cuddled up like a couple of kids.

# Sixteen

Tattoo shops have a wide variety of clients. We have the rough and tumble bikers, criminal elements, lawyers, doctors, and soccer moms. Most people are open-minded and generally have a free spirit. We see body parts and have tattooed all body parts. Most tattoo artists are not shy people. We get asked to tattoo literally every part of the human body that can be reached.

Many people who get tattoos in the genital region have no problem walking around naked and showing off their tattoos. It is like a woman that gets breast implants; they want to show everyone what they have. They like to show off their new titties.

Now everyone is not a free spirit, and some people are sheltered. That leads me to a funny story about a client and their friend.

It starts with a client of mine that is a stripper at an upscale place. She is a very free spirit but not a prostitute. She says she has never sold herself for sex and never will; that is just her choice. Anyway, she is having yet another boob job done. She is built like Anna Nicole Smith, a big-boned pale white girl with red hair and green eyes. She has an hourglass figure that women would kill to have. She has enormous breasts, and I might add, she has a huge husband that is six foot nine and built like a brick shithouse. He is a huge tattooed biker with a very open mind about what his wife does for a living.

So, I am tattooing my client, and his friend from a church youth group comes with him. My client is getting a cross tattoo with some scripture on his shoulder. His timid friend sits on a chair in my booth, watching his friend get a tattoo. Two very innocent boys at the age of eighteen. I would say they have never seen a pair of titties in person.

We are tattooing and discussing why the cross and scripture tattoo was meaningful. Earnest Christian conversation between these two and myself. I am nodding sure to their reasons and listening attentively. My red-headed client Lisa and her husband came walking in.

Lisa talks with Susan upfront, and Susan brings her back to see me. "Hey, Chris, Lisa wants to see you. Are you cool with that?" Susan smiles as she pokes her head into my booth. She sees the two young boys and gives me an evil wink.

Lisa comes into my booth in a tight top and tight boy shorts. She is wearing high heels and looks like she just came from a skin magazine photoshoot. "Hey, Chris, want to see the girls?"

I glance up at Lisa, and I look at the two boys. They look with their mouths open, stunned at Lisa. "Hell yeah, let's see the new girls."

Lisa pops her tits out, "Feel 'em!" I take off my gloves, and she leans over with her tits inches from my client's nose and lets me squeeze one. "They feel real, right?"

"Wow, those are great. Feels like the real thing. I bet Steve loves 'em." I look at my client, who is speechless; his friend looks like he has seen a ghost, has stood up and has backed into the corner of the booth. He has a boner and is trying to turn away to hide it.

"Hey, sweetie, you can feel 'em too if you want," Lisa winks at me as she walks towards the boy in the corner.

The boy looks like he is about to have a heart attack, "Um, no. I am, thank you, ok ma'am," he is stuttering and scared shitless.

Lisa turns to the client in the chair, "You want to squeeze my tits?" She holds out her chest to my client. He raises his hand and takes a quick squeeze.

"Holy shit. Those feel great." My client stutters. I laugh because I think the boy came in his pants.

Lisa's husband, Steve, is standing at the door of my booth, "Now, just one squeeze, little man." He laughs at the scared boys.

Susan takes Lisa and Steve back up to the front. Steve leaves some references for his upcoming tattoo appointment.

The boys are talking a mile a minute about Lisa's tits. They are asking if that happens here all the time and are those real people, and what do they do, and are they here all the time. I am laughing because that memory will be burned into their minds until the day they die.

We finish the tattoo, and the boys leave the shop talking about how big that lady's boobs were and how one touched them, and the other didn't.

Lisa called me, "Hey, did you see the references for Steve's tattoo?"

"Yeah, they will give me a starting point. I am sure that Susan has Steve on the books for me."

"Yeah, she got him in on a cancelation in four weeks. Is that cool?"

"Sure, that is enough time. Tell Steve I will let him know when he can come to check it out."

"Hey, Chris, is that kid okay, hahaha."

"You scared the shit out of him."

"He was trying to hide his erection. Oh, shit, young guys are too funny."

"Yeah, you evil witch, I think my client came in his pants when he squeezed your tit. Hahaha."

"I almost feel bad, but then again, I can be a little bit aggressive. I was going to sit in your client's lap."

"Those boys will have a permanent obsession with red-heads now. You have ruined them for life."

Susan walks up behind me while I am on the phone, "If that is Lisa, put her on the speakerphone."

I put Lisa on speakerphone, "Hey, bitch, you scared the fuck out of that kid. Haha," Susan has an evil laugh when she is up to no good.

"Lisa, you and Susan are not allowed to hang out together anymore. And stop terrorizing my young clients." I admonish them both.

"I am just trying to drum up business, Chris; I have to pay for the girls somehow; Steve ain't going to pay for them. Ok, he paid, but it is like a return on investment kind of thing. Haha"

"Shit, Lisa, we should get paid for guerilla marketing. Those boys will be lifelong strip club members." Susan walks back towards her office, "Bye bitch." Susan yells as she shuts the door.

"Ok, Lisa, I got Steve down for his appointment. I will talk to you later."

We hang up, and I think about the stories those boys will be telling their friends for years. I just got them addicted to ink, and Lisa started them on addiction to red-heads with big tits and round asses.

The tattoo scene is not always exciting. We get tired of the trends of fairies, hearts, tribal, armbands, Taz, and a million other fads. Sometimes the days are bland vanilla pudding for months, and then you get a really cool tattoo that you can make all your own. You design and draw it from your own skull. That is cool art that lasts and excites your motivation to do more.

Sometimes excitement comes in the form of the everyday grind. Like you are doing your 13th fairy of the week or your 13th nautical star of the week, and then some big dude passes out and pukes all over the place.

I had this big bastard come in, and he wanted a heart with mom in the middle of it. It was about four by four inches, not huge, just a quick heart with mom in the middle of it. Bread and butter tattoo, a little banger. So, I am almost finished with the tattoo. All I had left was some red on the top right of the heart. Bam, the big ass dude, passes out and crashes to the floor. I am sitting there looking at him; Troy brings over some smelling salt and wakes the dude up. We sat him back in the chair and brought him some chocolate candy and orange juice. He drinks the juice and then picks up my washout cup and drinks that. He gets a weird look on his face and vomits all over my tattoo machine, ink caps, floor, chair, and everything else. I jumped up in time, and he missed me with his vomit comet. He gets so embarrassed that he bounces out of the shop without finishing his tattoo. He paid before the tattoo, so I didn't care. He never came back to get the tattoo finished, either. What a douche bag.

# Seventeen

Troy and I ride to the shop on our bikes as usual. Every one says it looks like Sons of Anarchy and the Mayans riding together. Troy is this blonde, blue-eyed guy from Amsterdam, and then there is me, a dark Mexican with brown eyes and black hair, riding our Harleys down 101. We are both covered in tattoos. We back our bikes against the shop on the sidewalk in front of the windows. The engines rattle the windows, and our new manager comes out complaining about the noise.

"You are going to break the windows!" Mary goes back into the shop.

Troy raps the throttle a couple of times for good measure. "That should get her goat, Chris!" He climbs off his bike.

I push the door open and yell, "Daddy's home, kids." Rick and Mikail start screaming like chimpanzees, and Troy and I join in. It takes a good three minutes for us to all calm down. Mary makes the mistake of letting us know it makes her angry. She will learn the hard way, just like John learned, and Susan.

"Hey, Rick," I yell across the shop.

"Yeah, Chris," Rick yells back.

"Hey, remember that time that we got the apprentice and the piercer to do the milk challenge?"

"Hell, yeah, I sure do. We should get another apprentice and another piercer just so we can do that again!" Rick starts laughing.

"What is this milk challenge thing?" Mikail makes the rookie mistake of asking us about it.

"No way, Chris! The Ruskie doesn't know!" Rick is excited. I go running into Rick's booth. Troy knows what is going on, and he follows me into Rick's booth. We plan out our milk challenge for Mikail when Susan arrives at the shop. Mary runs up to Susan, and they have a little pow-wow.

"Chris! Come into the office, please!" Susan is standing at the doorway of her office.

"Oh, shit. I think I am in trouble." We all laugh, and I go to Susan's office. Susan reams me out for the idea of doing the milk challenge.

"We cannot have any cancellations, Chris. You cannot do this to Mikail. If it was an apprentice, I would be okay with it as long as I was here to watch it go down. For the record, we will not be getting an apprentice or a piercer, so those options are off the table."

"Damn it, we wanted to have a little fun." I hang my head in mock rejection.

"It would be helpful if you told Mary and Mikail what this milk challenge is so in the future they know." Susan looks at me.

"If you want Mary and Mikail to know. You can tell them yourself." I walk out the door of her office. Susan knows I am in a playful mood.

Mary comes by my booth, "That is fucked up, Chris. You were going to do that to Mikail?"

"Apparently, you have no sense of humor, Mary."

Mikail comes over to my booth and asks me about the milk challenge, and I show him a youtube video of it. He laughs and says that it was a funny joke. Mikail goes back to his booth.

I finish the drawing I am doing for Steve. I go talk to Rick, "Miss Mary 'Fun House' over here and Susan 'I have no humor' said we can't do it because Mikail would have to cancel his appointments."

"Aw, no fun, man. I remember when we used to do all kinds of fun shit." Rick smiles at me. "Hey, remember when we used to mix ink?"

"Hell, yeah. We destroyed some motel rooms doing that." I sit down in Rick's booth. Troy comes into Rick's booth to hang out as well.

"Chris and I used to rent a motel to mix ink because it was so messy. One time, Chris mixed up some green and left it on the blender for so long that it blew up. There was green ink all over the wall and ceiling and cabinet of the little kitchenette in the room."

"What the hell," Troy was laughing, "Did you have to pay for the damages?"

I start laughing, "Hell no, we gave them fake names. We left that shit there and took off."

Susan knocks on the door frame of Rick's booth. "Sorry for ruining your prank, guys."

"It is okay," Troy answers her, "you are the boss now like John was. Like a shop mom keeping us kids in check."

We all nod our heads, we all repeat, "Like a shop mom."

"Hey, Mom, I am hungry." I break up the temporary sadness of missing John. "I guess we all had to grow up at some point. I'm glad you did it! Hahaha. Better you than me," I walk out of the booth and pat Susan on the shoulder, "Suckerrrr."

Anne shows up with my daughter Patricia. The shop comes to a standstill when they visit. Anne asks Susan to go to lunch and then asks me if I can go. I am free to go to lunch, and Susan takes the rest of the day off shopping with Anne and our princess. I follow them to a nearby restaurant for lunch. When lunch is over, Anne and Patricia give me kisses. They all go shopping, and I go back to work.

Mary, the shop manager, calls me and tells me my appointment is there. For the last ten years, I have been tattooing butterflies on the butterfly lady, Tammy. She is covered with butterflies all over her body. She says she will shave her head soon to tattoo them on her head.

I pull up to the shop, and she is sitting out front with tight-fitting daisy duke shorts. She has a tube top struggling to keep her big tits inside it. She has on pink cowboy boots. Her blonde hair cascades down her back. If she was facing away from you, you would think she was a young girl because of how she dressed and her body shape. She is seventy years old, and her bright blue eyes sparkle from her wrinkled face. Her makeup is thick and bright, almost clownish.

"What's up, pretty lady?" I skip over and give her a big hug.

"Hey, you sexy man." She plants a kiss on my cheek. "Are you ready to tattoo some more butterflies?"

"Always. Where are tattooing today?" I ask because I have no idea. There is not much room left.

"I want one on the palm of each hand. So it opens and closes its wings when I close my hand." She winks at me.

"Holy shit! That is going to hurt!"

"You know me, I don't give a shit. Can't be a pussy when it comes to beauty." We laugh as we go into the shop to do the tattoo. I grab the shop help and tell them they will have to help me keep Tammy's hand open while I tattoo it.

Palm tattoos do not stick very well. They fall out, and you have to stipple them into the skin. That means straight down into the skin of the palm. It is excruciating, and it will most likely fall out anyway. You have to grab the thumb and the pinkie finger and force the hand open while you tattoo it.

Tammy proves to be a tough old bird like I knew she was. She sits through the tattoo on both palms and acts like nothing. I can't understand it. Great pain control. She decides that she wants one on her ass when we are done. A wing on each butt cheek because she saw it in a skin magazine.

"Tammy, I don't have time to do that today."

"Can you at least outline it today? I will come back in and get the color another day?"

"Okay, just the outline, though. I don't have time to fill in the black on the wing edges either, just the outline."

"Okay, sweetheart. Whatever you can do."

She drops her daisy dukes, and it is no surprise that she has no panties. She lays down on my table. I make a tracing of one cheek and then mirror the design and make a stencil. I use a nine-round liner and blast the outline for her butt-er-fly tattoo. When we are finished, she yanks up her shorts and pays on her way out.

"I made an appointment to get it finished, sexy man."

"Ok, see you then, Tammy baby."

Anne and Susan show up with a car full of shit they bought while shopping. Of course, they had to buy my "tattoo princess" Patricia many new outfits. I laugh at how spoiled my daughter is going to be.

# Eighteen

Our shop help is this tiny little Korean college girl that is twenty-one. Her name is SI-Woo. I do not think she has ever drank anything alcoholic. She speaks excellent English, and her Spanish is not bad. She is timid, and I don't know if she will be able to deal with this business. She is doing a good job so far; she is just very quiet. She is taking a break from college for a year before doing her master's program. She hopes that the tattoo experience will help her with her anthropology studies. She is scary smart.

Troy is from Amsterdam and is the biggest pothead you will ever meet. He smokes every day and has for many years. His new thing is chocolate chip cookies that are edibles. He bought some today and has a bag of them in the back.

Mary comes to my booth looking for Si. "Chris, have you seen Si-Woo?"

"Nope, Mary. She was helping me earlier, but I have not seen her for a couple of hours." I stopped to think about it, and it had been four hours since I saw her. "Where is she?"

"That is what I am asking you. No one has seen Si-Woo for several hours. Her car is out front." Mary is concerned because she is a tiny cute Asian girl in a rough neighborhood. We all stop what we are doing and look for her. Troy goes across the street to the store, but she is not there. We are looking everywhere for her, and no one can find her. Finally, Mary Calls her phone. We can hear SI-Woo's phone ringing. Mary hears the phone in the storage room in the back of the break room. We go look, and there on the massage table in the back under a blanket is Si-Woo.

Mary pulls the blanket off and asks Si-Woo if she is okay. "Yes, I am just so tired."

"Did you eat anything? Maybe you need to eat?" Mary brings her some water.

"I ate two chocolate chip cookies." Si-Woo almost whispers.

"Oh! Shit? Someone her size should only eat half of one!" Troy is amazed.

"God damn it, Troy. Now you get to help me take her home. You will have to follow me to her house and bring me back. Dumb ass." Mary stomps out of the room, and she calls Susan.

"OOOO, you are in trouble." I tease Troy as I walk by him. "Nice to see ya; I wouldn't want to be ya."

All of us rib Troy about how Susan will chew him out. Maybe even fire him.

Troy comes by my booth as Mary gathers up Si-Woo's stuff. "Hey, Chris, Susan won't fire, right?"

"No. But Susan is going to chew your ass. I can guarantee that."

Troy and Mary leave to take Si-Woo home. He has to follow Mary to Si-Woo's apartment and then listen to Mary all the way back to the shop. I think that should be punishment enough.

The following day Troy stayed quiet in his booth. Susan came by, and she and Mary ignored Troy all day. It was Susan's way of letting Troy know she was pissed at him. The shop rule was no one was to be visibly high or smell like they were high or drunk. Troy had always kept it under wraps for all the years he had been with them. This was his first and only mistake.

Si-Woo did not make it in today, and Susan let Troy know that was his fault. She also told Troy that he would be the shop bitch today and every day until Si-Woo returned. Troy was depressed about it, so he called a friend who is a body modification artist. The body mod artist is Christine. She works out of a big shop in downtown Los Angeles. Their shop is the one that does all the body suspensions, implants, and exotic things like that. Christine comes in and visits for a bit.

"Christine, why are you over here?" I am curious as to why she came into my shop.

"Troy says he is depressed. He wants me to implant some silicone pearls under the skin on his dick to give it bumps for extra pleasure for the ladies. Hahaha." She points to Troy standing at the door of his booth in his underwear.

"Come on, Christine, before I lose my motivation." Troy pats his junk.

"Well, have fun with that, Christine. Better wear double gloves because I don't think that Troy knows where his dick has been."

"Come on, Chris, that is mean. I know where my dick was last night. In your mom." We all laugh at Troy.

"So, you been sticking your dick in the dirt again?" Troy realizes my mom has been dead for years.

"Well, you know what I mean fucker." Troy turns and sits down on his reclining tattoo chair and pulls off his underwear.

"You could let me get set up first. Jesus Troy." Christine laughs at Troy, who is impatient to do the procedure.

Christine and Troy are busy with Troy's dick implants. Susan and Mary go to Troy's booth to talk to him. "God damn Troy, why you got that Vienna sausage tiny dick of yours out.

Are you trying to get an extension? Hey, Christine." Susan crosses her arms at the door of the booth and watches. "Mary, are you seeing this?"

"Jesus, what are you guys doing?" Mary covers her mouth with her hand.

"Christine, this is Mary. Mary, this is Christine. If you want implants, Christine is the one to do it." Susan stays and watches Christine work.

Mary turns and leaves, freaked out by the procedure. Mary goes to the front desk as a customer comes in.

"Hey, Chris, someone here to see you," Mary calls for me.

A friend and a client Jake Smith. He is always bringing me things to buy or trade out for tattoos. The last time Jake came by, he brought me a stainless Ruger Redhawk 44 magnum pistol. He gave me a great deal on that one, and it only cost me three hundred dollars. Today Jake brought me an AK-47 with a fifty-round banana clip. He says it is full auto. I wanted to buy it so bad, but I told him no thanks with Patricia in the house now. Rick bought it from Jake for five hundred bucks! What a steal. Illegal as hell, but what a steal. Rick will throw in a hand-sized skull tattoo on Jake's shoulder.

George and Mikail come running into the shop laughing. They are huffing and puffing from running.

"What the hell are you two doing?" Susan asks.

"Tutu Dude has been sleeping behind the dumpster," Mikail says out of breath.

"And?" Susan is worried.

George answers Susan, "So, I gotta shit really bad, so Mikail and I go out to the dumpster."

"He shit on Tutu Dudes fucking bed. Right in the middle of it. Holy Shit, that was funny."

Mikail doubles over laughing.

"I was going to tell her! Damn it, Mikail." George socks Mikail in the shoulder.

"Mikail has pictures to prove it, Right buddy?"

"Yes, right here is the proof," Mikail holds out his phone.

On the phone is George taking a dump on the bed, then there is a picture of the dump in the middle of the bed.

"Oh, shit, I gotta go wipe my ass." George runs to the bathroom.

"You two are sick in the head." Susan shakes her head and goes back into the office.

"I thought she would like it because she was mad at Tutu?" Mikail acts all letdown.

We all laugh about it. We look at the pictures some more and laugh. It is never-ending dumbassery around here. I am sure that the bed will just get flipped over, and they will keep sleeping on it.

Christine finishes with Troy's implants and puts two stitches on each of the ten holes she made with a scalpel. She inserted round silicone pearls under the skin and then sewed them closed. "That will be a little sore, Troy. No sex for two weeks! No jerking off either, dumbass."

"Ok. I promise. How long is it going to be sore?" Troy walks gingerly to the door of his booth. There are bloodstains on his underwear.

"At least a week. See you later." Christine says her goodbyes, takes her bag of stuff, and leaves.

Troy gets dressed and sits in his booth. Mary goes to talk to Susan about Jake making a

trade with Rick. Susan tells Mary that she will charge Rick the standard percentage Rick

pays the shop.

# Nineteen

Anne comes to shop with Patricia every week to see her auntie Susan. The three girls go shopping and go to lunch. Susan and Anne have become family. As far as Patricia knows, Susan is her aunt. I am so happy with how life is going. Alicia is doing well, John Jr. is in college doing well, and Tammie is a straight-A student in her senior year. Our family has weathered the storm, and we are sailing on smooth seas.

The shop and the corporation are booming. Susan is killing the game with all the shops, and the corporation is raking in cash. Susan set up Alicia and the kids as well. Sam has helped us invest in other buildings and properties. We have started to purchase the properties where our tattoo studios are located. John would be proud of how far things have come.

Patricia, my daughter, is crawling and creating havoc at the house. Anne is a great mom and a fantastic wife. I have been sober. Susan is training Troy to take her spot, and Susan is taking on more significant projects. I joke around that we are the tattoo mafia. Susan has flooded our market with artwork, stickers, hats, clothing, and toys. Our artists design and draw everything. If you designed it, you get a more significant percentage of the sales as an incentive.

We are all in, and it seems like we are unstoppable. It blows my mind how far we have come.

Anne pulls up to shop, rushes in with Patricia, and hands her to me. Susan knows something is up and watches as Anne storms by. A blonde lady comes barging into the shop, yelling at Anne. Anne is taking off her earrings and headed straight for the blonde lady. Susan watches excitedly to see how Anne handles herself.

"Look, you wetback, you can't drive twenty in a thirty-five and hold people up. We are not in Mexico." The blonde lady is shaking her finger at Anne.

"Oh, shit. Kick her ass, seabass," Rick yells from his booth.

Anne marches past Susan, right up to the blonde lady, and punches her in the mouth, "I have a child in the car, you crazy bitch." She knocks the lady on her ass. Susan pulls Anne back from the lady on the floor.

"I am pressing charges. You're going to jail," the blonde lady screams at Anne.

Susan leaves Anne with Mary, goes to the Blonde lady, and offers to help her up. "Come on now, sweetheart, you cannot think that you can come into a person's place of business and act like that." Susan holds her hand out to the lady.

"Get away from me, you black bitch!" Rick runs up and grabs Susan before she can beat the shit out of the blonde lady on the floor.

Susan calls Officer Torres and explains what is going on. He shows up with two squad cars and comes into the shop. The blonde lady is still on the floor screaming obscenities and racial slurs at Susan and Anne. Officer Torres speaks to the lady and tells her that he will view the video and charge the criminal responsible. He asks her if she needs anything. She refuses any other help, so he has her go outside and fill out a police report.

"Jesus, you cannot let her get away with this shit." Susan is wound up.

"It will be okay. Let me see the video." Jesus and Susan go into the office and watch the parking lot video and inside the shop. "Susan, let me go outside and talk to the lady."

Jesus goes outside and informs the lady that he has her on video trying to hit Anne's car coming into the parking lot. He also has her on video yelling racist remarks at Anne and Susan. He explains that he will not press charges for assault with a vehicle, trespass, and a hate crime because of the things the lady said before and after Anne hit her. Jesus explains that the ladies will not press charges if the lady leaves and does not come back. If she disagrees, he will arrest her on charges he mentioned to her.

The lady is angry, but she keeps her mouth shut. She gets into her car and leaves. Jesus comes back in and asks if everyone is okay.

"Why didn't you arrest her?" Susan is angry. "You are just going to let that white soccer mom come in here and attack us?"

"Well, for starters, Anne cannot assault people. So, I am trying to keep Anne from being arrested for assault. Two, you know that yelling racist shit is not a legal excuse to hit someone. Third, there was nothing on the camera to show she tried to hit her with the car. I made it up. So relax." Jesus stood there with his arms folded across his chest. "You can say thank you now."

Susan stood there with her mouth open, speechless.

"Thank you, officer Torres," Anne said, "I am sorry." Anne came over to Patricia and me and hugged us. "I am sorry, Chris, I am not going to let some bitch attack my family."

"You did well. Wow, what a spicy bitch. Damn, you hit hard." I laughed at her. I have never been prouder of my wife.

Susan thanked Jesus. She told him that she would fix him a good dinner tonight when he came over. We all joked around about the fight and kept telling and retelling our favorite parts. Anne's fight became a legend in the shop.

All the police left. Susan, Anne, and Patricia went on their day of shopping. I tag along and go to lunch with them like I do once in a while.

Everything good comes to an end…

Mary goes into Troy's booth, "Have you seen Chris?"

"He is not back from lunch with Susan and Anne?"

"Well, his appointment is here. What do I tell them?"

"Hold on, I will call him." Troy tries Chris's cell. No answer, "He is probably riding over here now from lunch. Tell them he will be here in a few minutes."

Mary goes back to the front and tells the client that Chris is on his way here. They have a seat and wait.

Susan calls and tells Mary that Chris has been in a bad accident on his bike. Officer Torres called Susan and Anne to go to the hospital.

Mary closes the shop, and they all meet up at the hospital. When they get to the hospital, they find that there has been no word on his condition. All they know is that he was hit by a black SUV. The SUV left the scene of the accident.

An hour later, the hospital informs them that Chris has died from his injuries. He never regained consciousness.

Officer Torres informs Susan that the SUV pushed Chris off the road and left the scene. They have no other information on the accident.

**Vengeance Is Mine**

What happens when our family is violently taken from us? What would you do to protect those that you love? How would you go to make sure that you paid the criminal back for the unforgivable crime of murder? Come take a ride with Steven a family psychologist that is married with a wonderful daughter and a storybook life. Watch in horror as Steven embarks on a dark journey of vengeance to obtain revenge for the death of his family. Do you agree with him as he vows to make the murderer pay for the violence committed to his family? Experience his slide into being the monster that he tries to execute. Steven's dark journey illustrates the dangers that can consume a soul full of hate and grief. Come and take a ride with Steven as he careens out of control in this chilling story of vengeance. It is what many of us would want to do, but Steven shows why revenge is a dish best eaten cold. What starts as a noble cause turns out to be the reason that we are told that "Vengeance is Mine" says the Lord. Bad guys look out. This quiet-spoken sissy boy doctor is on the prowl, and you are his target. Introduction I believe that the human species is one of the most violent species on the face of the planet, yet it also can be the most compassionate. How is it that such extremes can exist within a species? Is violence part of our instinctual nature, and compassion a part of our intellect? Or is it the other way around? I am never amazed at the actions of which humans are capable. At times, it seems as though the species is no more than a rabid animal. The talk shows, reality programs, cop shows, and all the material that flood our minds with violence and hatred seem to reduce us to our primitive beginnings. Rarely is love and compassion shown to the extent that the other negative aspects of humanity are shown. The negative and base emotions draw the ratings, and so does sex. If humans are not animals, then why do we act like animals? Many people in law enforcement will tell you that humans can be the vilest of creatures. I am not saying we are all that way, but I believe that even Robert Luis Stevenson knew this about humanity when he wrote, Dr. Jekyll and Mr. Hyde. The world religions all speak of the dangers of vengeance and revenge. It is a fruit that is best left uneaten. This book leads you on a journey with Steven R. Parks into the depths of human compassion and hatred as a warning to all of us who sit on that fine line of civilization rooting for revenge for the acts of violence committed against us. With that said, enjoy the story, and remember that "Vengeance is mine," says the Lord


**Suffer the Children. Porfis the Patron Saint of Karma**

The reason that he was called Porfis is so sad. However, that is life. It is what it is. That phrase was burned into his mind. Porfis said it all the time about anything traumatic and brutal. His true name is Jesus Christian Porfirio Escalante. His mother is a devout Catholic, and so that is why she named her boy Jesus Christian Porfirio. The nickname Porfis came from the traumatic murder of his mother. The murder was committed by his father in front of Jesus. His father told him to beg harder to save his mother's life. So, the little boy Jesus became known as "Porfis." It was because when the coroner came to take his mother away, the little boy, with his mother's blood running down his face, was still screaming, "Porfis papa, porfis," short for "Por Favor."

The murder had happened in Puerto Palomas, Chihuahua. Thirty-plus miles from Deming, New Mexico. The murder is known well in Mexico and the southern states of America. It was famous because of the brutality of the murder in front of a child. It became a thing of legends, like "Candyman" or "La Llorona." Poor Porfis never had the chance of having an everyday life. His father was killed in a shootout with the Federales that came to the murder scene. Porfis lost both his parents that day. He never thought about his father; he did not care about that evil man. "Porfis," thought about his mother every day. The smells of blood, and gasoline, and the chainsaw. The salty iron taste of her blood in his mouth. The scream of him, his mother, and the scream of the chainsaw echoed in his head as background noise to his daily life. Some people like to say that time heals all wounds. Time makes grief bearable. They were wrong. Porfis suffered every day of his life. It was as real today as it was 30 years ago. That little eight-year-old boy "Porfis" remembered everything. How could he forget? He had a photographic memory. Jesus survived by trying to separate himself from Porfis as a coping mechanism.

As traumatic as that sounds, Porfis grew up to be a quiet boy. He did well in school and was well-behaved. He made his Abuela proud as he served as an altar boy. Porfis attended seminary, and instead of being a priest, he became a teacher. He worked as a youth pastor at an Episcopal church. It made his Abuelita happy. Porfis hid his trauma well. He also hid his experiments with grief therapy well. The animal experiments helped Porfis with the trauma of life that he so cleverly hid over the years.

Porfis had to deal with bullies in his family and life at school, church, the store, and the park. He had a way of dealing with bullies in a very subtle way. So subtle that they never knew Porfis was the driver of their karma. The bullies never connected the two. Porfis is seen as a weak and broken thing. Never did people see him any other way but a broken spirit. All the years of charitable deeds went unnoticed. All the challenging work of helping others went by without so much as a thank you until Porfis became the harbinger of karma.

Other less fortunate souls would find Porfis out and tell him their stories and ordeals. When they confessed their trials to Porfis, karma found a way to make things right.

**Four-Claws**

Blaine "Four-Claws" Swanson was an adopted Native boy from a reservation near WestPoint, Ca. He was adopted to a family in Modesto, Ca. to help hide the boy from his past until it was time for him to come into his own and lead. Blaine must go through many horrors in life to be ready for his coming role in the tribe. The harrowing journey takes him through the survival of serial killers, Ng and Lake, and the knowledge of the sky people. He is not ready for this. A surprising out-of-this-world tale about the watchers of old and the protectors of now.